Martha, giggling, caught Duncan's eye. He grinned at her eagerly. Once, a long time ago, they had promised each other always to be friends like Mum and Uncle Harry. But Uncle Harry had never drowned Mum's doll. Martha scowled at Duncan and looked away. She laughed and whispered with cousin Mary. She took slow, tiny bites of her haggis, to make the delicious taste last longer. She looked everywhere and smiled at everyone but Duncan. She filled the hollow space in her stomach with almond-cream and sweetmeats.

Somehow, though, the hollow space seemed to be growing larger. Martha ate until she had eaten too much, and her stomach felt uncomfortably full. But right on top of that was the aching empty spot. She wanted everything to be like it had been yesterday, when Lady Flora was in her arms and there was all the excitement of Hogmanay to look forward to. Now that Hogmanay was here, Martha felt cheated. She should be having more fun.

By Cynthia Rylant:

OLD TOWN IN THE GREEN GROVES
Laura Ingalls Wilder's Lost
Little House Years

The Rose Years
Laura's daughter, born 1886
LITTLE HOUSE ON ROCKY RIDGE

LITTLE HOUSE
IN THE HIGHLANDS

by **MELISSA WILEY**

HarperTrophy®
An Imprint of HarperCollins*Publishers*

Special thanks to Caroline Carr-Locke for digging up detailed information about customs and cultures in late-eighteenth-century Scotland, and much gratitude to Norman Kennedy for his wonderful recordings of Scottish folk music.

Little House in the Highlands
Text copyright © 2007 by HarperCollins Publishers

www.littlehousebooks.com

Library of Congress Cataloging-in-Publication Data
Wiley, Melissa.
    Little House in the Highlands / Melissa Wiley. — 1st abridged ed.
        p.   cm.
    Summary: An abridged version of the childhood adventures in the Scottish countryside of six-year-old Martha Morse, who would grow up to become the great-grandmother of author Laura Ingalls Wilder.
    ISBN-10: 0-06-114817-2 (pbk.) — ISBN-13: 978-0-06-114817-0 (pbk.)
    1. Morse, Martha—Juvenile fiction. [1. Morse, Martha—Fiction.
2. Wilder, Laura Ingalls, 1867–1957—Family—Fiction. 3. Family life—Scotland—Fiction. 4. Scotland—Fiction.] I. Title.
PZ7.W64814Li 2007   2006103479
[Fic]—dc22   CIP
                                                                AC

Typography by Christopher Stengel
❖
First Harper Trophy edition, 1999
Abridged Harper Trophy edition, 2007
22 23 24 25 26 LBC 18 17 16 15 14

For Scott,
who makes the hills and valleys roar

CONTENTS

CONTENTS

The Friendly Valley

Loch Caraid was a small blue lake tucked into a Scottish mountain valley. On its shore were a half dozen cottages that had no names and one stately house that did. It was called the Stone House, and a little girl named Martha Morse lived there with her family many, many years ago.

The name of the valley was Glencaraid. That meant "Friendly Valley," and Loch Caraid meant "Friendly Lake." The people who lived in the valley had a story about those names. One summer evening, when it was just cool enough for a fire made of peat grass to flicker on the hearth, Martha heard the story from her mother.

Martha's three brothers and her one sister were downstairs in the kitchen begging plums from the cook. Her father was busy at his writing table. Father was laird of the estate of Glencaraid, and he had important letters to write. So just for now, Martha had Mum all to herself in the cozy corner beside the hearth of Mum and Father's big bedroom.

"It was many hundreds of years ago," Mum was saying, "that a man named Edward MacNab caught his first glimpse of the loch from high above on the mountainside."

Martha scooted her stool closer to Mum so that she could hear better above the spinning wheel's hum. Beneath Mum's fingers, golden brown flax fibers twisted into one long, spider-thin thread.

Mum's tale spun out above the thread. Edward MacNab, she told Martha, had been traveling for a very long time. He was bone tired and hoped to see the smoke of a chimney in the valley below, for he had a longing to spend the night in a warm bed.

But the evening was misty and dim. All Edward could see of the valley was the dark water of the lake at the foot of the mountains. In the gloomy light, it looked exactly like a mouth waiting to swallow anyone who dared climb down. Not far from the lake were two little ponds that looked just like two angry eyes.

"'Tis no a friendly sort of a place, that!" said Edward McNab. He spoke aloud, for he thought there was no one around to hear. But he was wrong.

A water fairy lived in the lake, and she had wandered onto the mountain that evening to gather mist from the rocky crags. When she saw Edward, she wrapped some shreds of mist around her so she wouldn't be seen. And she would have stayed hidden, if only he had spoken more wisely—or not at all.

"But it is ever the gift and the curse of a MacNab to speak the thoughts that pop into his mind," Mum told Martha. "Your father has it, and so do you, my bold wee lass."

"But what about the water fairy?" Martha said impatiently.

"Well," Mum went on, "it did not sit well with the fairy to hear this stranger speaking of her loch in that way. She crept up to Edward and, quick as a wink, she turned him to stone.

"'Not friendly, is it?' she said to Edward—for though his body was frozen in rock, he had yet the senses of a man and could hear her."

Mum's lilting voice grew cold and furious as she spoke the fairy's words. "'Who are you to judge this loch?' Inside his stone skin, Edward MacNab quaked. He wondered if he would spend the rest of his days as a boulder on this mountain."

"Did he, Mum?" Martha asked, then shook her head thoughtfully. "Nay, he couldna have. I've never seen any boulder up there that looks like a man."

Mum laughed. Martha was the youngest of the five Morse children, but Mum said she was sharper than a new pin. "Well, this water fairy was kinder-hearted than many of her race. She told Edward he would be under the spell for just a year and a day. 'You shall stand here sunup and sundown,' said she, 'and watch this loch in all its moods. We will see then if you can say it is not a friendly sort of place.'"

"A year and a day! But that's a terrible long time!" Martha interrupted, and then clapped a hand over her mouth.

"Aye," said Mum, winking at her, "but not so long as forever."

Then Mum told how Edward MacNab had had to sit frozen on the mountain through all the long days and weeks of a year.

The worst of it was, not a single day had passed before Edward knew that the water fairy was right. When the sun rose the next morning, he saw before him a lake bluer than the sky. Wind-ripples danced across it. Golden light glinted off the lake and the two small ponds nearby. The heather on the hillsides was a purple the like of which Edward had never seen before. Even the gray and craggy mountains were no longer forbidding, but seemed instead like gentle guards keeping watch over the lovely loch and its valley.

At last the year and the day had passed. The fairy returned and laid a hand on Edward's stone shoulder. Instantly he was flesh once more.

"'Tis right you were, miss, and I beg your pardon," he said. "I'm of a mind to end my travels right here—if it be all right with you."

The fairy was pleased, and she said that he might stay. So Edward built a house in the valley, and in time, he found a wife to live in it with him. And he told his children the story of the water fairy, and they told their children. And so it went for hundreds of years, until all the people around knew the lake as Loch Caraid, the Friendly Lake, and the valley as Glencaraid, the Friendly Valley.

"But, Mum," said Martha when her mother had finished the tale, "what happened to the two little ponds that looked like eyes? There aren't any ponds in the glen."

"Och," said Mum, "there's a tail to the story.

The fairy didna want anyone else thinking those ponds looked like staring round eyes, spoiling the pretty view of the valley. So she rolled up the two little ponds into a linen sheet and shook them out into Loch Caraid!"

Martha couldn't see how you would go about rolling up a pond in a linen sheet without all the water soaking through, but everyone knew that fairies had special tricks of their own.

"I've never seen any fairy in the loch," she said. "Is she still there?"

"The Good People are wary," said Mum. "You'll not see them unless they want you to."

Martha made up her mind that she would see that fairy someday, sure as water was wet. As soon as she was old enough to go out in the rowboat with her brother Duncan, who was her best playmate, she would go looking for the beautiful green-haired lady.

But she was only six and a half, and Duncan had just turned eight. Father said they could not go out in the boat alone until they were much older. Half seven seemed plenty old enough to Martha, but Father was firm. And what Father said went, for he was Laird Glencaraid.

Everyone in the valley was under Father's care. He owned all the land north to the tip of the valley and south almost to the village of Clachan. That land had been in his family for hundreds of years—ever since Edward MacNab built his house there, in fact.

Father had inherited Glencaraid from his MacNab grandmother years ago, before Martha was born. Her older sister, Grisie, had been just a wee girl when the title passed to Father. Her brother Alisdair had been the tiniest of babies. Now Grisie was fourteen, nearly grown up, and Alisdair was twelve.

Robbie, who was eleven now, had been born the year Father began to build the new house. Duncan was the first baby born in the Stone House, in Mum and Father's big bedroom above the parlor. Martha was born there, too. She liked to climb into her parents' big bed with the green plaid curtains that hung round it and try to remember being a tiny baby in Mum's arms. Try as she might, she could not remember it.

But now it was nearly time to go to her own bed in the nursery. Grisie and the boys came clattering up the stairs, munching the last of their plums. Robbie had a half-eaten plum in each hand. As he came into the room, a third plum slipped out from under his arm and rolled across the floor.

"Oops!" he said to Martha through a juicy mouthful. "That one was yours."

Martha fished her plum out from under a chair. It was bruised, but just a little.

"Here, Martha," Duncan said, offering her a new plum. "You can have mine."

"Nay, this one's all right," she said. She smiled at Duncan. He always stuck up for her when Robbie teased. Everyone said Duncan and Robbie looked so much alike they could be twins, except for the three years' difference in their ages. But although they had the same thick brown hair curling on their necks and the same dark-lashed blue eyes, they were really nothing alike. Robbie was bold and loud, and he had something to say about everything. Duncan liked to keep his thoughts to himself around most people. He had a calm, steady gaze that Cook said was wise as an owl's and twice as uncanny.

Martha bit into her plum. It was tangy sweet and delicious. Duncan and Robbie were taking turns tossing their plum pits into the fire. When Martha had finished eating, she threw hers in, too. Grisie sat quietly on her stool, taking small, careful bites. Robbie could eat five plums in the time it took Grisie to eat one.

Alisdair ate slowly, too, but it was not because he was neat. He was in fact always a little rumpled, with his red hair falling into his eyes. He held a plum with one big bite taken out of it in one hand, but he had picked up Father's copy of *Scots Magazine* and was leafing through it, forgetting to eat. The magazine came by post all the way from Edinburgh several times a year. Sometimes there were stories in it, and Mum or Alisdair would read them aloud to the rest of the family.

At last Mum rose from her spinning.

"Get into your nightclothes, and I'll be right along to tuck you in," she told Martha. She said the same thing every night. It gave Martha a nice comfortable feeling to hear those words.

Martha picked up her doll, Lady Flora, from the cradle beside Mum's bed. Martha had slept in that cradle when she was a tiny baby, and so had her brothers and sister. But now they all slept in the nursery.

Martha crept to Father's side to say goodnight. The light of an oil lamp on the writing table spilled over his close-cropped red hair. His white wig with the tightly rolled curls rested on its stand beside the table. Father looked up from his letter and smiled at Martha.

"Have you had your fill of stories for one night, then?" he asked.

"Oh, no, Father. I still want to know where Edward MacNab found his wife, and what the water fairy does with the mist she gets from the mountain."

Father shook his head in mock dismay. "Och, Martha Gráinne Morse, the Judgment Day could be upon us and you'd stand there spouting questions about what happens to the sheep when the farmers go to heaven!"

"But what *will* happen to them, Father? I'd like to know."

"Aye, and I'd like to know how many days my men have to cut the peats before it rains. You'll never find as many answers as you have questions, Martha."

He gave her a kiss. Martha held up Lady Flora for her own kiss, and Father solemnly brushed his lips against the wooden cheek.

Martha went across the hall to the nursery. She snuggled in next to Grisie, ready to dream about stone men and green-haired ladies and sailing with Duncan on a glittering, friendly lake.

THE STONE HOUSE

The first sound Martha heard each morning was the bang of a box-bed door sliding open. All the beds in the nursery had wooden walls built around them and wooden ceilings on top, so that each bed was like its own tiny room. Alisdair had a box bed all to himself, Robbie shared with Duncan, and there was a third bed for Martha and Grisie.

At night, after Mum tucked Martha in and gave her a kiss, she gently slid the bed's door-panel closed. It was very dark inside, but it was warm and cozy.

The loud bang that started every morning was Robbie in a hurry to get out of bed. After the door banging and the slapping of Robbie's feet on the floor came the soft sound of the housemaid's humming. Martha always waited in bed until she heard Mollie enter the nursery. Martha loved to listen to the old Gaelic work songs and ballads that hung in the air around Mollie like birds. Like her brothers and sister, Martha could speak Gaelic as well as English, and she thought songs sounded prettier in the ancient language of the Highlands.

The smell of warm porridge had filled the air along with Mollie's song. Martha slid open the door-panel and climbed out of bed.

The good porridge smell chased the last sleepiness out of the room. Now everone was awake and eating. Breakfast in the nursery was a standing-up affair. Robbie stuck his finger in the cream-pot, and Grisie stalked to the fireside to scold him. Ever since their governess had gotten married and moved away two springs ago, Grisie acted like she was in charge of the nursery. She would be fifteen in the fall, and Mum said she could put her hair up then. Right now, Martha liked to watch it sway from side to side when Grisie walked. She would be sorry when Grisie began to wear it twisted up off her neck.

Alisdair and Duncan went behind the tall wooden screen in the corner of the nursery to get dressed. Robbie went off to Father and Mum's room to see if there was any porridge left from their breakfast. While the girls waited for their turn behind the screen, Grisie sat down on the hearth to brush Martha's hair.

"The fairies must have been here last night," Grisie told Martha. "They've tangled your hair into a dozen elf-locks! If you'd keep your nightcap on, they couldna get at your hair, you know."

"I dinna take it off on purpose," Martha said. "It comes off when I'm asleep." Her toes found a hole in the floorboard beneath her.

After Grisie was done with Martha's hair,

she helped Martha into her blue plaid petticoat and dress and tied her dust-gown in the back. The dust-gown was like a long cotton apron with sleeves. Martha didn't like to wear it, but Mum said it kept her dresses from getting too dirty.

Grisie did not have to wear a dust-gown. She never got a spot on her dresses, not even the white ones. She tied a sash below the bodice of her yellow linen gown, which had once been a dress of Mum's. Last spring it had been cut down to fit Grisie. Martha ran to Mum's room next.

Mum was just stepping into her petticoat. Mollie helped her tie the laces. Since Mum was not expecting visitors today, she put on only a plain linen everyday dress.

Mum finished dressing and said she must look over the food stores, for it was nearly time to send Father's steward, Sandy, to town to buy sugar and spices. Martha went down the stone staircase to the kitchen to see if Cook was baking pies today.

The Stone House was the only house in

the valley with an upstairs and a downstairs. It had stone walls and a gray slate roof and smooth wooden floors. There were two chimneys, one on each end of the roof. Upstairs were the nursery and the bedroom, and downstairs were the big kitchen and the parlor.

Martha wandered into the kitchen. Today was not a pie day, after all. There was no piecrust on Cook's table, nor any sweet baking smell in the air. There was only the rich brown smell of the broth that was always simmering. The huge fireplace ran along the west wall of the kitchen and there were three long benches set into the earthen floor around the hearth, where the servants sat to eat their dinners.

Tucked into the back corner of the kitchen, next to the staircase wall, were Cook's bed and washbasin. Mollie shared a bed with Nannie, the kitchen maid, up in the attic among rolls of handspun yarn and chests of linen. Sandy lived in one of the cottages on the lakeshore with his wife and his seven children. He came to the Stone House early every morning to do chores and to answer the door when visitors came.

"Good mornin' to ye, Miss Martha!" Cook smiled at her from one of the benches by the hearth, where she sat shelling peas. She was a large woman with a round red face and a stubborn chin. Her gray hair was hidden beneath a tight white cap that made her red face look even redder.

Martha climbed up beside Cook and sat for a while, swinging her feet back and forth, back and forth, and every now and then sneaking a pea from Cook's bowl.

"The broth wants stirrin'," Cook said. "Happen ye'd like to do it?"

"Aye!" Martha cried. It felt very grown-up to stand before the fire and stir the soup in the big black cauldron. Bits of onion and a bundle of sweet herbs bobbed to the surface, like little fish showing their heads in a pond.

Martha loved to sit in the kitchen with Cook and listen to her stories. Cook had worked in a castle before she came to Glencaraid, long ago when she was a young girl.

Cook said she would not work in a great house like that again for all the world. There had been one hundred and seventeen stairs, and they all had to be scrubbed once a week. The silver service was so large that it took three girls two whole afternoons to polish it.

"And hungry all the time, I was," she told Martha, "for nivver was there enough for the servants to eat. The worst of it was, we all had our meals in the dining hall at one great long table. The laird's family sat up at the head, and the servants sat at the foot. Heaps of fine food we'd bring out from the kitchen, and all of it went at the head of the table. Roast beef, fresh butter, bowls of plums and apricots, and always a big platter of oysters from the sea loch. Down at the foot where my place was, all we had was barley cakes and a weak broth. Bitter hard it was, to gnaw on an old stale cake with the smell of roast beef floating down from the head of the table!"

Cook shuddered, remembering. "Ye mind me words, Miss Martha," Cook said. "'Tis better to live in a little house where there's no more work than can be done in a day and decent food for everyone, than in the finest castle in the county, where every soul has either too much or too little than is good for them!"

"I'd have made them give you some beef," Martha told Cook hotly.

"Och, the little dear!" Cook said. "I've no doubt ye would have—if ever ye'd had occasion to notice me, that is. Ye wouldna have been allowed to sit in the kitchen worritin' the maids with yer questions, that I promise you! Made to keep their distance from the servants, the young ladies of that house were, except to order us about. Ye'd have been a different person had ye grown up there, Miss Martha!"

Martha frowned. She did not understand how a house could make you a different person.

Cook had finished with the peas. Martha grabbed a last handful out of the bowl and ran outside to look for Duncan.

She found him down near the farmers'

cottages, just beginning a game of Babylon with some of the tenant children.

"Miss Martha!" called Annie Davis. She was one of Sandy's daughters. She stood opposite Duncan on the grass, both of them holding their arms high and clasping hands to make an arch for the other children to walk through. But when Annie saw Martha, she said, "Ye must be Queen, Miss Martha."

"Nay, she's too little," said Annie's brother Johnny.

"I am not!" Martha cried indignantly at the same time that Duncan said, "No, she isna!" Annie made a face at her brother, and gestured for Martha to take her place opposite Duncan.

Martha stretched as tall as she could to make the arch with Duncan. Then Annie galloped underneath, and Martha and Duncan dropped their arms, trapping Annie between them.

Annie chanted the words of the game:

"How many miles to Babylon?"

Duncan and Martha chanted back:

> *"Threescore and ten."*
> *"Will I be there by candlelight?"*
> *"Yes, and back again."*
> *"Open your gates and let me through!"*
> *"Not without a beck and a boo!"*
> *"There's your beck and there's your boo,*
>   *Now open the gates and let me go*
>   *through!"*

As she said the last verse, Annie gave an imaginary coin each to Duncan and to Martha, the King and Queen. They raised their arms again, and let Annie gallop through.

The game made the morning pass quickly, and before Martha knew it, it was dinnertime. The farmers' children all disappeared into their cottages for the meal, and Martha and Duncan raced up the hill to the Stone House.

If there was company, dinner was in the parlor. But on most days it was upstairs at the oak table in Mum and Father's bedroom. The bedroom was for eating in, and working in, and living in. It was there Mum sat to spin and tell stories after supper. It was there Father sat in his big chair and read from the newspapers that came by post from Edinburgh.

Alisdair read everything Father would let him. They would talk for hours about the new plows farmers were using in England, or about the trouble brewing in France, or about what was happening in America, the brand-new country across the sea where the people had fought a great war because they did not want to be ruled by the British king.

Martha liked to hear them talk about America best of all. Alisdair had told Martha that America had won its War for Independence in the year 1783, just one year after Martha was born. Martha had been spellbound—a whole country that was nearly the same age as a little girl! Why, Scotland was thousands of years old. She did not understand, exactly, how a country could be so young.

At dinner that day, Father said he would go to look at his trees in the afternoon. On the west side of the valley, he was raising hundreds of young trees from seed. Before Father, there had been hardly a single tree on the whole estate—only some twisted pines on the mountains and a few fruit trees in the kitchen garden. Now there were two whole plantations of fir and larch.

"You should see them, Margaret," he told Mum. "As tall as your waist now, and branching out splendidly. In another year, we'll have quite a little wood down there." He broke off a piece of bread.

"When those firs I put in behind the garden get big enough, they'll break the wind in winter and shade us in the summer. I've half a mind to put in a row near Gavin Tervish's cottage. Now that he's a father, I'm thinking it's more worried he might be about the cold drafts whistling through the cracks in his walls."

Grisie gave a delighted gasp. "A father! Did Mrs. Tervish have the baby, then?"

Martha put down her fork, too excited to eat more. It was always grand news when a new baby was born on the estate.

"Aye," Father said. "Did I not mention it? A fine lad was born this morning before dawn, and both mother and bairn are doing fine. Auld Mary was there for the birthing, of course."

Martha knew Auld Mary was the old woman who lived away out on the moor, the great open stretch of land beyond the end of the lake. Auld Mary knew about every plant that grew, and made potions and ointments for all the people of the valley. Whenever a baby was born, Auld Mary was there.

Mum spooned up the last of her pudding and pushed the dish away from her. "Well! We must get to work, girls. We'll have to fix up a basket of gifts for the bairn. I wasna expecting it quite so soon."

Grisie squeezed Martha's hand under the table. That meant they would pay the baby a visit tomorrow. Martha couldn't wait.

THE NEW BAIRN

The next morning, Mum, Martha, and Grisie set off for Gavin Tervish's cottage, with the basket of presents they had packed. Martha ran ahead, leading the way down the hillside. They passed the cowhouse, the stable, and the sheep-yard. They passed the carriage-house and the mains, where the unmarried farmworkers lived. The men with families had their own cottages on the lakeshore, just down the hill and around the bend.

Like all the farmers' cottages, Gavin

Tervish's was a long, narrow house built of turf, big squares of grass that had been cut from the moor and piled one on top of the other like bricks. The roof was thatched with broom-grass that was bunched into thick, watertight bundles and fastened onto the roof beams.

In the middle of the roof was a flat square of slate held up by four short legs. It looked like a little hat on top of the house. The slate covered a hole that had been made in the roof for smoke to come out, since there was no chimney. In bad weather, rain could not beat in and put out the fire, because of the little slate hat.

There was no door, so the entrance was always open to the sun and wind. Martha could see inside to the round fireplace in the middle of the floor. Mrs. Tervish smiled at Martha from a seat near the fire. On her lap was a bundle of sheeting with a tuft of dark hair sticking out the top.

Martha liked the Tervish cottage. The house was divided into three rooms by two inner walls. There was the tiny bedroom at one end, the kitchen in the middle, and a place for the cows at the other end. The inner walls did not go all the way to the roof, so that light and smoke could drift from one end of the house to the other.

The cows were out at pasture now because it was daytime. Only Mrs. Tervish and the new baby were at home, and old Mrs. MacFarlane, who was Jeanie Tervish's mother. There was a fierce, proud gleam in Mrs. MacFarlane's eyes today as she sat knitting rapidly.

Mum and Grisie followed Martha into the cottage. Mrs. Tervish greeted them warmly and began to rise, murmuring something about getting a cup of tea for her ladyship.

"Nonsense," Mum said, smiling. "You just sit back down and rest." Before Mrs. Tervish could say a thing, Mum had drawn a bench next to her chair and was cooing into the sheeting at the little red-faced baby.

"Such a fine young mannie he is," Mum said.

"Aye," said Mrs. Tervish in a soft voice,

"he's a bonny one, he is."

"Jeanie Tervish!" said Mrs. MacFarlane in a shocked voice. "Mind yer tongue, lass! Do ye want to tempt the Wee Folk to steal your babe oot of yer varry arms?"

Without slowing a stitch in her knitting, the older woman rose and peered out the doorway. For a long moment, she looked all around. Then she went back to her seat in the corner, shaking her head dourly.

"I dinna see any fairies, but that doesn't mean that be none there. They'll snatch yer bairn quicker than a squirrel steals a nut, if ye gang on shoutin' to the warld how bonny he be." Her voice dropped to a whisper on the last words and she frowned fiercely at the baby, as if to scare his handsome looks away. But he did not look so very bonny to Martha, with his scrunched-up eyes and wrinkled red face.

"Here now, I've a gift for his wee self," Mum said. She opened her purse and took out a silver coin. Mrs. Tervish nodded gratefully and unwrapped the bairn a bit to free a chubby hand. Mum gently opened the baby's fingers and placed the coin in his fist. He gripped it tightly for a moment, then waved his hand and let the coin fall to the ground.

"There now!" Mum said, pleased. "He'll grow to be a generous man. That's a grand sign, Jeanie."

Mrs. Tervish looked proud and happy. Martha knew that if the baby had held on to the coin, it would have meant he would grow up to be selfish and miserly. All mothers were nervous when the first visitor placed the silver coin in the baby's hand. Martha wondered if she herself had dropped the coin when she was newly born. She hoped so. She would not like to be a mean, stingy woman when she grew up.

There were all kinds of precautions that must be taken with a new baby. No one must carry fire out of the house until the child was at least a week old. To do so would be very bad luck. So would speaking the name the child was to be given until after he was christened. The minister himself must be the very first person to say the baby's name aloud. Mr. Tervish would have to write his son's name on a slip of paper and hand it to the minister just before the ceremony.

Mum signaled to Grisie, and Grisie stepped forward shyly, carrying the basket. "We brought a few other tokens for the bairn," she said, setting the basket on the dirt floor beside Mrs. Tervish's chair.

"Och, 'tis far too kind ye are!" exclaimed Mrs. Tervish. "'Tis mair than enough ye came to see the child." She looked flustered and happy.

Mrs. Tervish looked at Grisie. "Happen ye'd like to hold him while I peek in yer basket?" she asked. But Grisie's eyes went wide with fear.

"Och, nay! He's such a tiny thing. I'm afraid I'd break him in two!"

"Well, I'm not," said Martha. "I'd like to hold him."

Mum laughed, and so did Mrs. Tervish. Grisie looked embarrassed, but Mrs. Tervish smiled at her.

"To be sure, I ken how ye feel, Miss Grisell," she said. "I did be thinkin' the same thing when Auld Mary put him in me arms yesterday mornin'. But once yer hands touch a bairn they seem to ken just what to do, all on their own."

"Sit yourself down here, young miss," Mum said to Martha, patting the bench beside her. "Is it all right with you, Jeanie?"

"Of course, Lady Glencaraid," Mrs. Tervish said. Carefully she placed the bairn in Martha's outstretched arms, and Mum showed Martha how to steady the baby's head and neck with one arm while the other arm kept snug under his little body.

Martha stared down at his head with its tiny smudge of a nose and the perfect little red bow of his mouth. She wondered how on earth she could ever have thought he wasn't a bonny baby.

Mrs. Tervish slowly unpacked the basket of gifts. Wrapped in a fine linen napkin were a dozen currant cakes and beneath them a large wedge of cheese. Beneath the cakes and cheese was a bottle of home-brewed ale for the new father, and a soft woolen blanket woven of thread Mum had spun herself. Mrs. Tervish shook her head admiringly.

"Ye have but to look at it to see who had the spinning of it," she said. "But, ma'am, it's far too fine for the likes of—"

"Nonsense," Mum interrupted. She hated such talk. So did Martha. She did not like to think of the estates where the laird treated his servants and tenants poorly, where any bairn would not be warmly welcomed.

After a while, the baby began to fuss. Mrs. Tervish said he was hungry and took him back so she could feed him. Mum rose and said it was time to be going. Martha hated to leave. But outside, on the way back along the lake path, Mum took a napkin-wrapped bundle out of her pocket and handed it to Grisie. Inside were three little golden cakes, glistening with ruby jam.

"Currant cakes!" Martha cried. "You saved us some!"

Grisie gave one to Martha and one to

Mum. They walked slowly up the path, eating the cakes. When Martha had licked the last of the jam from her fingers, she wiped her hands on her dust-gown and ran the rest of the way up the hill. A little wind came tickling up behind her, and it carried with it Mum's laugh and Grisie's soft voice. Martha thought of the tiny bairn she had held in the cottage. It had never yet felt the wind or tasted a currant cake. Martha was glad she was a girl getting bigger every day, and not a baby anymore.

THE BROWNIE

O ne morning when Martha woke up,
Mollie was already in the room, dish-
ing out the porridge. The sun was shining
through the nursery windows with all its
might.

Martha felt glad, and she danced a little
dance on the floorboards. But Mollie said,
"Och, I'd tread lightly today if I was ye, Miss
Martha. Cook's in a fearful dark mood, and I
doubt her poor nerves can take a pounding
from the ceiling."

"What's wrong?" Martha asked.

Mollie looked grave. "Forgot to leave the brownie his supper last night, she did."

"She never!" Grisie gasped. Martha could only stare. In all her life she had never known Cook to do such a thing.

A brownie was a tiny, tiny man who lived in someone's house and did little chores if he was left bits of food, and played tricks if he was not. Cook said the Stone House brownie was named Tullie Grayshanks. She said he had moved in as soon as the last slate was put on the roof, and he had been there ever since. He scared hawks away from the hens and made sure the foolish hens didn't lay eggs outside the chicken-house. If a button or needle was lost in the house, he'd find it and leave it where someone would be sure to see it. Cook said he helped herd sheep, cut hay, thresh oats, and do all sorts of other things around the farm. No one had ever seen him do those things, but Cook said he was there doing them just the same, and if you paid attention you would see that there was always more hay stacked than the farmers had cut.

Martha had hunted all over the house, but she had never seen Tullie Grayshanks. Martha had searched behind every cabinet and peered inside every mouse hole, but Tullie must always have heard her coming.

Every night Cook put out a little dish of cream and a round cake of oat bread called a bannock. She left them by the kitchen door and they were always gone the next morning. She said brownies were sensitive things and you had to be very careful not to upset them, or else the brownie would turn into a boggart, and he would play terrible tricks all over the farm. He would tie up the horses' manes in knots, and he'd make their horseshoes fall off. He would stop the hens from laying eggs and the cows from giving milk. He would creep into the kitchen and set the fire roaring so high that the bannocks would burn. There was no end to the mischief a boggart could do, when he was of a mind to.

Cook said one sure way to offend a brownie was to forget to leave him his supper. And now she had gone and done just that!

"Is Tullie Grayshanks angry, then?" Duncan asked.

"'Tis no for me to say," Mollie said. "But when Cook woke up this mornin', all the milk in the dairy was curdled. And not only that—yer mither's good china platter was lyin' smashed on the parlor floor, sure as I live."

"The brownie did that?" Martha wasn't sure she wanted to go downstairs, if there was an angry brownie about.

Mollie shook her head. "I canna say. It could be that I stood the platter wrong on the shelf when I put it away last night. Happen it tipped off balance and fell in the night. I canna blame the brownie when just as likely it was me own fault. But Cook says no one can blame me for curdlin' the milk, and she says she ought to pay for the platter, as it's her what riled up the brownie."

Alisdair slid open the door of his bed. "I dinna believe there is any brownie," he said in his matter-of-fact way. "That's just a story for children."

"Alisdair!" Martha cried, shocked.

Duncan said, "Then who eats the bannocks every night?"

"One o' the sheepdogs, most likely," Alisdair said. "They're always roaming about at night. And I should think it's the barn cats that drink up the cream."

"Whisht!" scolded Mollie. "Mind yer tongue, Master Alisdair."

Alisdair shrugged. He never minded if people did not agree with his ideas.

"What will we do if Tullie goes on being angry, Mollie?" Martha asked.

"Och, there's no tellin'. But Cook is downstairs now, mixin' and stirrin' for all she's worth. She aims to leave him some special little cakes wi' his cream tonight. She says happen Tullie will forgive her, seein' as it's the first and only time she's ever forgotten him."

The porridge wasn't very good this morning. Cook had put in neither sugar nor salt. Martha ate as much as she could stand, and then Grisie helped her get dressed. Martha took Lady Flora and went down to the kitchen to see if she could help make the cakes. Duncan came, too.

"Happen she'll let us lick the spoon!" he said.

But Cook hardly glanced at them when they came into the room. She was beating eggs in a bowl, stirring so fast and so hard that her knuckles were white on the spoon.

"Good morning to you," said Martha, feeling rather shy.

"Ye may call it that if you like," Cook answered crisply, not looking up from her bowl.

Martha and Duncan looked at each other. Duncan's eyes said to Martha, *Let's go out to the garden instead.*

Aye, let's, Martha's eyes replied.

Almost tiptoeing, they went through the kitchen and out the back door. Martha stood a moment feeling the warm sun on her skin. The garden was a soft, wet, glittering world of green and silver. Sunbeams melted on the whitewashed stone walls of the dairy, the little low building just behind the Stone House. The dairy was where the milk and butter were kept and where the churning was done.

Duncan went to pick some plums from the trees at the edge of the garden and Martha followed him slowly, feeling the mud squelch between her toes. The kitchen garden was enclosed by low stone walls and ringed with rows of pear and apple trees. It was laid on a flattish part of the hill, where the slope was very gentle. At the far end, helping to block the winds that swept down off the mountain, was a line of buildings: the ale-house, the laundry, and the dove-cote, where pigeons were raised. The pigeons made a constant cooing noise that was like water rushing over stones.

A hawk circled overhead and Martha felt a sudden pang of fear for the little chicks in the hen-yard, on the other side of the garden wall. Who would look out for them if Tullie Grayshanks did not? Martha wished she could talk to him and tell him not to be angry with Cook.

"Yah, yah! Go away, you auld hawk!" Martha yelled into the sky.

Duncan laughed. "He's no after the chicks,

you goose," he said. "He's after mice in the oat field."

But Martha yelled again, "Yah, go on with you, hawk!"

If the hawk heard, he did not show it. He went on soaring in lazy circles, thinking his own private hawk thoughts.

After a while, Mum walked out through the garden, with barley cakes and cold sliced chicken, and a big tumbler of milk for Martha and Duncan to share.

"Your father is dining at South Loch today," she explained. "Wants to see how the rains have hit the oats there, he does. So I told poor Cook not to worry about a big dinner for the rest of us."

The children sat on a garden bench beside Mum to eat their dinner and Martha thought there could not be any nicer way to eat, sitting here with Duncan and Mum and Lady Flora in the sunny garden corner. For a moment, she felt almost glad that Cook was so out of sorts that they had to eat out-doors—but not really glad. She didn't want

Cook to be unhappy.

"Will Cook or Mollie have to pay for your platter?" she asked.

"Nay," Mum said. "'Twas no one's fault it fell. Happen someone slammed a door too hard and it made the cabinet shake."

"Or happen the brownie did it?"

"Aye, happen so."

"Will the brownie forgive Cook after he eats her cakes tonight?" Martha asked.

Mum smiled. "Wouldna you?"

Martha thought of Cook's delicious cakes. "Aye," she said. "That I would."

She knew then that it would be all right. Tullie Grayshanks would not turn into a boggart, nor would he leave Glencaraid. He would know Cook was sorry and would never forget him again. It was nice to have a brownie around the house, to find buttons and watch out for the chickens and keep Cook company in the lonely downstairs late at night.

A Surprise on the Road

One night Mum said the next day was Sunday and that it would be a kirk day, a church day. The whole family must get up early to go to Clachan, the little village across the lake. Father had arranged for the ferryman to carry them, for they would not all fit in the little rowboat. Martha was excited about the trip. The last time there had been a kirk day, she had not known about the water fairy. This time she would keep a sharp eye out, and perhaps she would see the beautiful lady with the long green hair.

The kirk in Clachan held services only once a month. The trip was too long to make more often than that. On the other Sundays, Father read aloud from the big Bible in the parlor, and he said prayers before dinner.

But today was not a usual kirk day. The Tervish baby was going to be christened and there would be a big feast on the grass outside the church after the morning service. Cook had been up since three in the morning, baking. Nearly everyone on the estate was going.

The sun had not yet begun to peek over the eastern hills when Father opened the front door and called for everyone to make ready to leave. Grisie hastily finished smoothing Martha's curls over the shoulders of her white muslin dress. Today Martha did not have to wear a dust-gown. But she mustn't get even the tiniest spot on her best Sunday dress.

Father was wearing his finest, too. He had put on the clothes of a Highland laird. He wore a coat of tartan plaid over his linen shirt. A wide piece of tartan cloth was belted around his waist and looped over his shoulder. This was called his kilt, and Mum had spun every bit of the thread herself. His jacket had gold buttons and wide, turned-back cuffs lined with silk. Red-and-black tartan stockings came up to his knees, and at the top of each was a golden tassel. On his head, he wore his bonnet, a large brimless hat with a knot of black ribbon tied round it.

He stood in the yard, looking down the hill toward the lake. A pale light was beginning to show at the corners of the sky. The air was quiet and still; there was no wind this morning. The valley was hushed, half asleep.

Then, so gently that Martha could not tell at exactly what moment it began, there came a high, sweet, reedy note, like someone singing.

It was the sound of bagpipes, and it grew louder and nearer. Sandy was playing, down by the lakeshore at the cluster of huts. Today he was not Father's steward—he was Father's piper. There had been a time when no

Highland laird would have gone anywhere, even across his own estate, without his piper behind him. But times had changed, and the old ways were fading. Today, though, was a special day and a time for celebration.

The pipes grew louder, and soon Martha could see the shapes of Sandy and his family coming up the path. Behind them were Mr. and Mrs. Tervish and old Mrs. MacFarlane. Mr. Tervish held the baby in his arms. He looked as proud as if he were a laird himself.

Behind the Tervishes came the rest of the farmers and their families, and all the servants who worked on the home farm. As soon as they reached the Stone House, they would all have to turn around again and walk back down to the lake, where the ferry would be waiting. But the new bairn's first journey must be uphill, for good luck, and so he was brought to the Stone House first. When Mr. Tervish reached the house, he bowed to Father and Mum.

No one spoke as Father led the way down the hill to the shore. Sandy's piping soared above their heads. Martha thought there was no sound in the world she liked better than bagpipes, except perhaps Mum's laugh.

At the shore the ferryman bowed to Father and Mum. His name was Mr. Shaw.

"Sit ye right here, miss," he said to Martha, helping her to a seat in the middle of the boat.

When the whole family was seated, the ferryman gave a great shove with his pole, and the boat surged away from the shore. Martha waved at the group of cottagers and servants left behind. The ferry would come back for them after it left the Morses on the opposite shore. It would have to make three or four trips to carry such a crowd.

Martha remembered to look for the water fairy. For a moment she thought she could see strands of green hair floating in the water just ahead, but the boat moved closer and she saw it was only a willow branch with long, pale leaves.

Sandy's bagpipes, fainter now, took up the notes of a psalm Martha knew well, and

Robbie and Duncan began to sing in loud voices.

Martha sighed. The fairy would hear them coming and hide for certain. She gave up searching and sang along with the boys instead. It was Sunday, and so they must sing only hymns, but God didn't mind if they sang them loudly.

The shore grew closer and closer until *bump*! the boat knocked against the grassy bank. Mr. Shaw leaped nimbly out of the boat and secured it to a wooden post sunk into the ground. He held out a hand to help Mum step onto the shore. Father picked Martha up and lifted her out of the boat.

"There you be, Light-as-a-Feather! Mind your shoes don't get wet!"

Martha's toes squirmed inside her boots. She wished she were not wearing them at all. Kirk days were the only days all summer when she had to wear shoes and stockings.

Father said they would wait at the shore for the carriage. He had arranged for one of his men to drive it around the lake and pick them up for the three-mile ride to Clachan. While they waited, Mum passed around bread and cheese for everyone to eat.

Then Mum said she had a surprise for Grisie. "Save a bit of that cheese and bread," she said. "Jeanie Tervish asked if you'd carry the bairn to the kirk."

"Me?" Grisie gasped.

Mum laughed. "Aye. You know the bairn must go to kirk in the arms of an unmarried lass. 'Twill bring luck to the babe if that girl is his laird's daughter."

Grisie's eyes shone. "I never thought about it," she said.

"I thought you were afraid to hold a bairn," Martha said.

"I'm not afraid. I was just caught by surprise that other time." Grisie tossed her head. "But Mum—how shall I carry the bread and cheese? I've no pockets in this dress!" Martha knew that the girl who held the bairn must carry with her something to eat, which she had to give to the first man she met along the way.

"Wrap them in a pocket handkerchief and pin them to your skirt," Alisdair suggested.

"Tie them to your head," said Robbie.

"Aye, with your hair ribbon!" Duncan added. The boys burst out laughing.

Grisie swept them a disdainful glance. Mum said, "The bairn will be in a basket. You can just tuck the bread and cheese right alongside it."

"Ah! Here's the carriage," Father said. Martha heard its wheels bumping before she saw it. Then it came around the bend, a small open carriage pulled by Father's two shaggy mountain ponies. "Who wants to ride?"

Martha and Duncan looked at each other. It was hard to choose. Father did not take out his carriage often, and a ride in it was a special treat. But it would be great fun to walk the road to Clachan with the Tervishes and Sandy and Cook and the rest.

"We can ride home," Duncan said.

Martha nodded. "Aye. May we walk, Father?"

"As you wish," Father said.

"But 'walk' means walk," Mum put in. "No berry picking, no footraces, and"—she looked hard at Martha—"no stains of any kind on your nice, clean clothes!"

Biting her lip, Grisie looked at her dainty slippers and her smooth, neat hem. "I suppose I ought to walk, too, if I'm to hold the bairn." The road would be dusty, and her shoes were sure to get scuffed.

"You needn't carry the bairn the whole way, Grisie. Only the last bit and into kirk," Mum reminded her. "Why don't you ride with us as far as the bridge, and you can wait there for the rest to catch up?"

Grisie smiled, relieved. "Aye, that suits me. Alisdair, you'll explain to Mrs. Tervish?"

Almost as soon as the carriage had rumbled away, the ferryman's boat returned. Gavin Tervish stepped out of the boat and lifted a rather noisy basket onto the ground. Martha rushed forward to peek inside. The baby looked so angry and helpless, with his red face and toothless gums, that Martha longed to pick him up. She wished Mrs. Tervish had asked her to carry him to the christening. After all, she was an unmarried girl, too!

"Not much of a sailor, is he?" said Mr. Tervish.

Mrs. Tervish hurried ashore and lifted the crying child out of the basket. "Hush, now. There did be no more rocking in that boat than in yer own nice cradle, so never ye mind yer fussin' . . ." Her voice was soft and crooning. The baby calmed and snuggled against his mother.

With a lot of chatter and laughter, the party set off along the dirt path toward the village.

Before she had walked half a mile, Martha's feet began to throb in protest. Mum had said she must not run or stain her dress, but she hadn't mentioned keeping her boots on. Martha knelt down and wrestled them off.

After that, the walk passed quickly. It seemed like no time at all before Martha spotted the footbridge. Beyond it, across the stream, rose the steeple of the little kirk in the village. Clachan was a small town, with only four shops plus the school and the kirk, but it seemed very large to Martha. There were twenty or more houses and a wide street running from one end of the town to the other.

"Look at her there, like a great pink rose," Mrs. Sandy murmured to Cook. Martha looked where she was pointing and saw Grisie waiting beneath a tree beside the bridge. Grisie looked so pretty and grown-up that, for a moment, Martha hardly recognized her sister. Martha quietly stepped aside to put her stockings and boots back on.

"Did Alisdair explain that I'd be waiting here?" Grisie asked Mrs. Tervish anxiously.

"Aye, that he did, and a sensible plan it was," Mrs. Tervish said.

"This is the bread and cheese?" Mrs. Sandy asked, nodding at a napkin-wrapped bundle in Grisie's hand.

"Aye," Grisie said. Mrs. Sandy took the bundle and placed it in the basket at the baby's feet. Then she put her hands on her hips and told Grisie she must not speak another word until they reached the kirk. And she must give the bread and cheese to the first man she met, no matter who it was.

"But dinna ye speak to him," warned Mrs. Sandy, "or ye'll bring ill luck upon the child."

Grisie nodded, looking as if she wished she'd never left home. But she held out her arm for the basket, and when she peeked in at the sleeping bairn, she smiled. Martha wished she had something to do, to help make the baby's life lucky.

Grisie led the way across the bridge into Clachan. The little crowd of churchgoers followed in a quietly chattering parade. Grisie was the only one who must not speak. Martha drew up beside her and talked and talked, because it was so funny to say things to Grisie when she couldn't answer back.

"I wonder what they'll name the bairn?" she said. "If I were a boy, they could name him after me." Grisie shot her a scornful look, but said nothing. Martha ignored her. "I suppose they could name him Martin, and that would be sort of like my name."

"Nay," said Duncan from behind. "They ought to call him Duncan, for me."

"You don't care a whit about bairns," Martha said. "He ought to be named for someone who appreciates him."

"Miss Martha, Master Duncan—ye're no pesterin' yer sister, are ye?" Cook called. "Ye mustn't distract her into speakin', ye ken."

"Och, nay, Cook," Martha said. "'Tis just keepin' her company we are."

Grisie rolled her eyes, but she could not say otherwise. Martha giggled.

They had walked halfway through town. The kirk was just at the end of the road. Father's carriage stood outside, and there was a great crowd of people at the door. Martha wondered how Grisie would decide which of them was the first man she met since she would reach them all at once.

Suddenly Martha realized there was a new noise mixed in with the noise of the crowd, a sound that should not be there. It was a great baaing and bleating that got louder and louder. It was a flock of sheep!

"What in the world?" Mrs. Tervish declared.

The noisy flock came trotting out from the lane and filled the road right in front of Grisie. Grisie's mouth was wide open but she remembered not to speak. The sheep filed around her, taking no notice of Grisie or the baby in the basket on her arm. Martha dodged out of the way of a large ewe who wanted to cross right where she was standing. Duncan was laughing, and so were a lot of the people gathered on the kirk steps.

"In heaven's name, who's got the keepin' of these sheep?" Gavin Tervish's booming voice called.

"I do," said a cheerful voice. "Sure and they're the luckiest sheep in all Scotland, for I am their master!"

A little man was suddenly standing right in front of Grisie, as if he had popped out of nowhere, like one of the Wee Folk.

Indeed, he looked like one of the Wee Folk, and people said there was fairy blood in his veins. His name was Peter MacBray, but everyone called him Brownie Pete, because he looked so much like a brownie, with his funny pointed beard and dancing black eyes.

"I heard there was to be a christening today," he said, "and I says to meself, 'Pete old friend, where there's a christenin', there's a percession, and where there's a percession, there's a bonny lass in front with jest enough bread and cheese to fill an old man's belly!'" He made a low bow to Grisie and took off his hat with a flourish.

"I do be kerrect in thinkin' I'm the first man ye've encountered on the road, miss?"

Grisie stared at him, astonished, and then she smiled. Behind her, Gavin Tervish burst out guffawing, and suddenly everyone was laughing. Brownie Pete had brought his sheep all the way down from the mountainside just to get a bit of bread and cheese. He was such a good shepherd that he would not leave his flock, but he thought nothing of herding them right through the middle of town and upsetting a whole christening party. Martha could see Mum laughing on the steps of the kirk, and even Father was smiling. The minister in his long robe tried to look sober, but his mouth quivered. Only Mrs. MacFarlane, the bairn's grandmother, did not smile. She glared at Brownie Pete. He didn't notice.

Grisie raised her chin. Even in the middle of the river of sheep, she looked regal. She made a graceful curtsy to Brownie Pete and, without a word, reached into the basket and pulled out the napkin of bread and cheese.

"Hee hee! Cheese from the laird's larder! 'Tis a fine day for an old shepherd. A blessing on the bairn, and a blessing on the lass!" He bowed to Grisie, and tucked the napkin into a fold of his plaid. Then, without another word to the christening party, he raised his staff and waved it at the sheep.

"Hey la, ye sheep of mine! Get ye on yer way to the green hillside! Hey la, sheep, ye've grass to eat!"

The sheep surged forward along the lane that crossed the main road. They passed between the houses on the other side to the open land behind the village. Brownie Pete waved his staff at a few stragglers, and then, as suddenly as they had appeared, the old shepherd and his sheep were gone.

The people on the road and at the kirk door burst into loud talk. It was a christening procession that no one would ever forget. Mrs. Tervish and Grisie hurried toward the church, for the bairn had awakened and was complaining about being stuck in the basket. Mum and Father moved forward to greet them. The minister waited at the top of the steps, smiling a welcome and looking relieved that the bairn had arrived without mishap. Mr. Tervish handed him a scrap of paper that had the baby's name written on it. The minister read the name silently, then smiled and nodded approvingly at Mr. Tervish. Martha couldn't wait to hear what name was on the paper.

"Bodes well for the bairn, it does," Martha heard Mrs. Sandy announce to a grim-faced Mrs. MacFarlane. "Brownie Pete is more than half fairy, or I'm a born fool. If yer grandson has his blessin' and the minister's both, he'll grow up free o' care. Ye canna ask for better than to be favored by both sides!"

"Humph!" was all Mrs. MacFarlane said, but her angry forehead smoothed out a bit.

After all the excitement it was hard to settle down into a Sunday kind of mood. Martha sat on her bench next to Mum and tried not to fidget or swing her legs. At last, the long sermon and all the long prayers were over, and the minister dripped water on the bairn's forehead and announced that his name was Allan Alexander Tervish. Father smiled, pleased. The Tervishes had decided to name their son after him. Then, just when Martha thought she would burst if she had to sit still one second longer, kirk was over and it was time to go outside for a celebration dinner on the grass.

A little way from the kirk was the town's bleaching-ground, where the women of the village laid out their linens to dry and whiten in the sun after washing them in the river. Today there were no drying linens; instead there were big tartan plaids spread out for people to sit on while they ate. Every household had brought something good to eat, in honor of the newly christened bairn.

Martha ate and ate and ate. There was sheep's-head broth and plum pottage, and stewed chicken and roast tripe, and cream sweetened with red-currant juice, and seedcake and shortbread and pie.

The christening dinner lasted nearly three hours. Then it was time to file back into the kirk. Since kirk was only once a month, the minister must squeeze in as much preaching as he could fit into a day. It was even harder to settle down for the afternoon service. Martha and Duncan took turns pinching each other to keep from falling asleep.

By the time kirk was over, the sun was low in the sky. Martha leaned against Mum in the carriage and watched shadows reach across the stream.

When the carriage drew up near Loch Caraid, the ferryman was waiting. The water made a lapping sound against the boat. The sound was like a lullaby, and Martha was asleep before the boat reached the other shore.

THE DUST-GOWN

I n August, it was time for the harvest. Even the farmers' children were needed in the fields. Some of the village children came across the lake to help, too. Martha and Duncan often walked out to the flax field to see if Duncan's classmates Lewis and Ian were there. Lewis Tucker's father was the blacksmith in Clachan, and Ian Cameron's father was the village weaver.

One morning when Martha and Duncan got to the flax field, Mr. Tervish told them that none of the village children had come today. The ferryman had taken his family to visit their granny in Lochearnhead, and the villagers had no way to get across the lake.

"Let's play Picts and Scots on the hill, then," Martha said to Duncan. Duncan shrugged and nodded his head.

The hill was called the Creag, which meant "pointed rock," and from the top, Martha could see the whole shore of the lake, from the Stone House at the other end to the stream at the foot of the lake that flowed south into big Loch Earn.

"I'll be the Scots warrior this time," she said as she reached the top of the wall, panting with the effort of climbing.

"Aye," Duncan agreed. He would play the Pict army, invading Martha's fortress. The Picts and Scots had been warring tribes who lived long, long ago, before Scotland was called Scotland. Alisdair liked to read Father's history books, and he had told Martha all about how the Scots had eventually conquered the Picts, and that was how Scotland got its name.

She and Duncan always played that the wall belonged to a Scottish chief, and his soldiers had to defend it against the wild Pictish army that raced up the hill shrieking terrible war cries.

Some movement on the Creag's rocky slope caught her eye.

"Robbie and Alisdair are coming," she called to Duncan.

Duncan frowned. Picts and Scots was a different game when Robbie played it. He was older and faster and stronger, so he always came out ahead in the battles.

"Wait for us!" Robbie yelled when he spotted Martha.

Martha sighed. They would have to choose armies now. It would work out evenly if Alisdair would play, but he never did. When Alisdair came to the hill, he spent his time looking for arrowheads or anything else that might have belonged to the ancient builders of the wall.

"We'll have to take turns, two against one," Duncan said.

Martha told Duncan and Robbie they could side together first. But Robbie only laughed. "Let a bit of a lass like you defend a post all on her own?" He shrugged at Duncan. "You can have her. I can handle the both of you." Still laughing, he ran to the bottom of the hill.

Martha stuck out her tongue at his back. They must win this battle.

Duncan took up a position next to Martha on the wall. Martha crouched on the corner post as if she were ready with bow and arrow for the attack. With an ear-splitting whoop, Robbie ran up the slope toward the wall. But Martha surprised him. With the wildest, loudest battle cry she'd ever given, she leaped off the wall and landed right on top of Robbie.

She heard Robbie make a funny whoofing noise, as if she'd knocked the wind out of him, and then she was rolling down the hill, the world going around her in a dizzy blur. At last she stopped.

"Martha!" Duncan yelled. He ran to her

side. "Are you hurt?"

"Nay, I think not," she said. She sat up slowly. "Just dizzy."

Duncan helped her to her feet. He winced at the sight of her dust-gown. It was streaked with dirt and grass stains, and there was a long ragged tear near the hem. Worst of all, she must have rolled over a fresh pile of cow dung.

Martha wrinkled her nose. She didn't smell very good. But then she thought of Robbie's shocked face and decided she didn't care.

She followed Duncan back up the hill. Robbie was sitting dazed against the stone wall, glaring at Alisdair, who was doubled up with laughter.

"Dropped you like a rabbit, she did!" Alisdair crowed.

"I'll drop you if you don't watch out," Robbie said sourly.

The shadow of the Creag was beginning to creep across the foot of the lake. It was one o'clock, time to go home for dinner. Martha and her brothers scrambled down the rocky path to the lakeshore.

Sandy was just leaving the yard, leading a horse toward the stable. Martha hadn't known Mum and Father were expecting company.

She and Duncan exchanged nervous looks. Father would not like a guest to see his little girl looking so dirty.

"Ken you whose horse it is?" she asked.

"The duke of Argyle's," Robbie said. "Better practice your curtsy."

Martha's heart gave a sick thud, but Alisdair said, "He's only teasing, Martha. Dukes don't drop in unannounced, with only one horse and no servants. That horse belongs to Laird Alroch."

That was better, but still, Father and Mum were not going to be pleased. Alisdair picked some grass out of Martha's hair and wiped a smudge off her cheek. But he could only stare helplessly at her dust-gown.

"Are they in the parlor?" Martha whispered.

Duncan and Robbie crept into the house to peek and came back quickly.

"Aye," Duncan said.

"Leave your dust-gown in the kitchen," Alisdair suggested. "Your dress is all right, isn't it? You can explain to Mum later."

That was a good idea. Martha pulled off the smelly, dirty dust-gown and wadded it up. She followed the boys inside. But before they reached the kitchen, Grisie called to them from the parlor doorway.

"Come on," she said. "Father's waiting. We have company."

"But we haven't washed up yet," Alisdair began.

"Then these two ought not to have stuck their big heads in the doorway!" Grisie retorted, nodding at Duncan and Robbie. "Saw you, Father did, and sent me to find out what's happened to your manners."

There was no hope for it. Martha would have to take the dust-gown into the parlor, with her. She didn't know if it would be worse to put it back on, or to carry it into the parlor, where dirty laundry did not belong. Holding the gown behind her back, Martha slowly trailed after Grisie and the boys into the parlor.

The parlor was a large, solemn room that was used only for company and holidays. In the middle of the room was the enormous, polished wooden table that Father's grandfather had brought from England.

There was a tall case of books in the corner, next to a little one-legged table, upon which rested the enormous family Bible. The parlor also had a sideboard and a china closet made of real mahogany. Against the staircase wall was an old box bed that had been in Mum's family for a hundred years. It was for guests to sleep in, when they stayed overnight.

Laird Alroch was standing at the hearth beside Father. He was a nice old man who lived in a stone castle on the other side of the mountain.

Suddenly Martha realized that no one was looking at her. There was a commotion of hugging and my-how-you've-growns, for Laird Alroch had not been across the mountain for a visit in half a year. No one had noticed Martha hanging toward the back with her crumpled dust-gown in her hands. She looked around wildly. The door of the box bed was open. She stuffed the dust-gown under the pillow.

Her heart pounding, she whirled around. No one had seen her. It had taken only a second. She was lucky the bed had been open. Usually it was kept closed.

Then Martha crossed to the hearth and kissed Laird Alroch's wrinkled cheek. Inside she was trembling. Suppose Mum asked why she wasn't wearing her dust-gown? She would have to tell everyone how naughty she had been. But no one asked. Laird Alroch tapped his breast pocket, where he always kept candies, and winked at Martha.

"Ye can take a peek noo, but we must leave them till after dinner or your good mither will have me hide!" he said.

"And speaking of dinner, here it is at last," said Mum. Mollie came into the parlor with a huge tureen of sheep's-head broth. She placed it on the table near Father's chair. Nannie came just behind her with a platter of potatoes and turnips.

"Tatties and neeps!" Laird Alroch beamed. "Me favorite!"

They all sat down and Father said the blessing. Then Mum filled Martha's bowl with the good, rich broth full of barley and vegetables. Martha ate every drop, and two slices of chicken, and a plate of tatties and neeps. The food was so good that Martha forgot all about the dust-gown.

She did not remember it when Father said he was glad Laird Alroch was staying the night, for he wanted to show him the larch plantation and the west turnip field that afternoon. She did not think of it once all the long afternoon, for Cook was making a chestnut pie and she let Martha help her take the stones out of the raisins and roll out the crust. Then Mum set Martha to work at her sewing sampler, and Martha had no thought for anything but the number of pricks she gave her finger with the needle.

Soon it was suppertime. Cook had made a good supper of cabbage and potatoes and savory roasted rabbit. Dinner was the big meal of the day, and supper was usually just broth and oatcakes. But tonight there were extra dishes for supper in honor of Laird Alroch.

After the dishes had been cleared, Father went to the fire and put another peat on the flames. He pulled chairs near the hearth for Mum, Laird Alroch, and himself. Martha, Grisie, and the boys gathered close on the hearth benches. The big ale cups were brought out, and a jug of ale that Sandy had brewed last winter. And Cook had saved some whey for the children.

Martha held Lady Flora in her lap and drank the whey, the part of the milk that got squeezed out when the milk was turned into curds for cheese making. It was cool and delicious.

The whey filling her belly made Martha sleepy. She thought she might like to curl up right there, beside the fire, like a cat. Lady Flora felt heavy in her arms. At last, Mum said it was bedtime. Martha held Grisie's hand as they went to the nursery.

It was not until Martha climbed into bed that she remembered the dust-gown. As she snuggled in next to Grisie and lay her head on the pillow, another pillow flashed into her mind—a fat feather pillow in a crisp linen pillowcase, with something dirty and smelly wadded up beneath it. The dust-gown was still in the box bed!

And Laird Alroch was sleeping there.

Martha cried out in dismay. She was wide awake now.

"What is it?" Grisie asked. "Be you sick?"

"Nay," Martha groaned. She did not see how she could have been so foolish. Why else would the box bed have been open, unless it were being aired out for a guest to sleep in? Why else would it have been made up with freshly bleached sheets and a fine, fat pillow? Pillows could not be left in the bed when no one was visiting, for mice would be sure to get in and nest in the feathers.

"Martha! Tell me what ails you!" Grisie

said. She sat up in bed, her eyes wide and worried. "Should I call Mother?"

"Nay, nay," Martha said quickly. "I'm not sick. I just remembered something, that's all."

Grisie snorted. "Ah, come to bed without washing behind the ears again, did you? Well, you'd best start remembering. I'll not be having all the dirt of the moor rub off your neck onto my pillow, do you hear me?"

Martha started to protest, then remembered that Grisie was right. She *had* forgotten to wash behind her ears.

"Aye," she muttered.

"We all hear you!" came Alisdair's muffled voice from across the room. "Stop your squawking, will you?"

Martha wanted to sleep, but she could not. She thought about kind Laird Alroch finding her dirty dust-gown in his bed. Or perhaps he would not find it, but would lie in the closed box bed all night wondering where the smell of cow dung was coming from.

Tomorrow, everyone would know how Martha had shamed her family. Grisie would never have done such a naughty thing!

Martha did not know when she fell asleep. She only knew that the night seemed very long.

Laird Alroch was to leave just after breakfast. Mollie came into the nursery and said the children were wanted in the parlor. It was a special treat to eat breakfast in the parlor, with Father and Mum and Laird Alroch. But Martha could not feel excited. She moved very slowly pulling her petticoat and dress over her head.

"Come on, Martha!" Grisie said impatiently. "We mustn't be late for a parlor breakfast!"

Martha wondered if Laird Alroch had already told Mum and Father, or if he would wait until Martha was there.

Martha walked slowly to the table. She sat down, and after a long while, she finally dared to look at Laird Alroch. The old man was watching her. His eyes twinkled at her. Very slowly, he winked.

Martha began to wonder if perhaps Laird

Alroch was not going to tell on her after all.

As soon as breakfast was over, he began to say his good-byes. He promised to come for a visit at the New Year.

At the very last, he stooped down to speak to Martha. "I have a boon to ask of ye, bonnie lassie," he said. "I've a bag of sweeties here that's weighing me doon. 'Tis glad I'd be if ye'd take it off me hands!"

Martha took the bag, and then put her arms around his neck. She hugged him, hard. He whispered something in her ear.

"If I were ye, I'd have a look underneath yer mither's china cabinet this mornin'. It looks as though the Wee Folk ha' been makin' mischief hereabouts, usin' yer clothes for their picnic blankets!" He winked at her again and then slowly straightened up. He climbed upon the loupin'-on stone to mount his horse.

Martha stood still, watching him ride slowly down the path toward the mountains. Duncan and Robbie ran beside his horse for a little while. Martha wanted to run, too, but she could not move. She knew she must go in and get her dust-gown out of its hiding place before Mollie went into the parlor to do her sweeping.

"Martha!" Mum said. Martha jumped. Laird Alroch had ridden out of sight. Mum was looking at Martha curiously.

"Is something amiss?" she asked. "You're staring at naught!"

"No!" Martha said. "I mean—I mean— aye." She looked at the ground.

Martha swallowed down the lump in her throat. In a very small voice, she told Mum the whole story—about ruining the dust-gown, and hiding it in the bed, and Laird Alroch keeping her secret to save her from disgrace.

Mum's face was grave. The smile that never left her eyes was buried very deep. But it was still there, a little. Martha did not feel quite as bad as she had felt all night.

"I think you know how naughty you have been," Mum said. "You should not have tried to hide your dust-gown. That was deceitful, which is a kind of lying."

"Lying!" Martha's eyes opened wide. "But I didna tell any lies—"

"Nay, not with words. But by pretending that naught was wrong, when you knew something was, you were telling a lie, just as surely as if you'd spoken it."

The lump was back, bigger now.

But Mum said, "I'll not go on about it. You understand now, do you not?"

Silently Martha nodded.

"Then the matter 'tis finished. Laird Alroch is a kind man. Not many would take such trouble to keep a small lass from a scolding she well deserves!" Mum put her hand on Martha's head. "Come. Let's see if a good soaking will take the stains out of that dust-gown. Then you can mend the tear." Martha nodded.

She went into the house with Mum, thinking about kind Laird Alroch. He had been nicer to her than she deserved. She wished she could do something for the old laird, to thank him. She made up her mind. She'd think of something.

Auld Mary

Every morning, Mum put Martha to work on her sewing. Martha sat beside her sister and struggled to make the stitches march along a straight road, as Grisie's did. Somehow Martha's always looked more like a winding mountain path. Grisie did everything better.

Martha wished she could learn to spin instead, but Mum said she was not big enough.

"You'll need a few inches yet before your foot can reach the treadle, me love," Mum said.

It was not fair being the youngest. Everyone could do things that Martha couldn't. Alisdair could read Latin, and he knew all about history and politics. Father said there was not a man on the estate who could outrun Robbie in a race. Duncan could carve whistles out of wood and he could draw birds and animals that looked almost real. And Grisie could sew and draw and read and write and do figures, and she could spin.

But Grisie had not learned to spin until she was eight. It occurred to Martha that if she could not do something *best*, perhaps she could do it *youngest*. After supper that night she watched closely as Mum sat at the spinning wheel.

The next day, Mum and Grisie were out of the house all afternoon on a visit. Martha went up to the bedroom to look at the spinning wheel. It was made of smooth, cherry brown wood and sat on three long carved legs. The wheel part was on one side, with a wooden rod connecting it to a pedal at the bottom. That was the treadle, which Mum stepped on to make the wheel revolve.

Martha could picture exactly how Mum sat in front of the wheel, pushing the treadle with her foot and holding one hand up to the bundle of flax. As the wheel turned, Mum's fingers kept drawing out strands of flax from the distaff and pinching them together so that they became one long continuous thread. The motion of the wheel caused the thread to wind itself around the bobbin. When Mum spun, it was like a kind of sitting-down dance.

Martha thought she would try it herself. She sat on the stool, but saw that Mum was right: her foot could not reach the treadle. So she tried standing up. She drew out several fibers from the bundle on the distaff, as she had seen Mum do. Then, pinching the fibers between her fingers, she stepped on the treadle.

The wheel spun quickly round. The bobbin turned and pulled the flax through her fingers. It burned a little so Martha licked her fingers the way she had seen Nannie and Mollie do, and took hold of the drawn-out flax fibers once more. She stepped on the treadle. Again the spinning bobbin pulled the thread through her fingers. She held on and watched the thread wrap itself around the bobbin. She was spinning!

But the wheel was pulling the thread too quickly. She could not hold the fibers tight enough, and the thread that wrapped around the bobbin was thick and full of fuzzy slubs. Her thread did not look at all like Mum's.

Perhaps it was much easier sitting down. If only her legs were longer. Mum had been right.

Martha wanted to grow and grow—not a tiny bit every day, but all at once. Now! She thought of someone to help her. Auld Mary knew all there was to know about everything that grew. She knew which herbs would cure sore throats, and chilblains, and toothache, and every kind of sickness. Perhaps she knew of an herb that made small girls grow more quickly, too. Some people even said Auld Mary was a witch. Surely a witch could help Martha to grow.

Martha set off at once. She cut across the heathery grass behind the farmers' cottages and ran all the way up the Creag. She had never gone so far by herself. Mum would not mind, as long as she did not go near the peat bog beyond Auld Mary's hut.

At last, there it was: a tiny mud-and-turf cottage with smoke drifting out of a hole in the roof. The cottage had a friendly sort of look about it. Tangled vines framed the open doorway, with a few late roses showing off their silken petals. An orange cat with white paws sat in the doorway, staring at Martha and twitching its tail.

Now that she was here Martha felt a little shy. She had known Auld Mary all her life, but it was different, somehow, coming here to ask for magic.

The cat opened its mouth and yawned a very wide yawn. Then it turned and went into the hut.

Martha followed it slowly. In the doorway, she called out, "Good day!" but there was no answer.

She took another step forward.

"Auld Mary?" she asked.

Auld Mary was not there. Martha and the cat were alone in the hut. It was a tiny house with just one dark room. For a moment, Martha could not see anything, but then her eyes got used to the dim light. She could see a spinning wheel, a water pail, and an earthen bench built against one wall. On top of the bench was a thick woven blanket spread out over a pile of straw. That was Auld Mary's bed.

Against another wall was a second bench. It held an empty dye pot, some dishes and bottles, and a small bag of meal. Slumped against the meal was a little muslin doll with no face. Martha remembered that Auld Mary sometimes made dolls to trade for meat.

A small iron pot hung from a hook over the fire. Something inside it bubbled gently. It smelled like potatoes. Beside the fire were two short-legged stools and one long bench, which had upon it two rough wooden plates and two cups and a dish of oatcakes.

Martha suddenly realized she was very hungry, even though she had eaten dinner not long ago.

"Ah, I see ye've caught yerself a mouse, Kitty!"

Martha turned at the sound of the voice. There was Auld Mary, wrinkled and bent and dressed in an ancient shirtwaist and a coarse gray skirt. A yellowing linen cap covered her head, and her plaid apron was faded and dull from many washings.

The cat ran over and rubbed against Auld Mary's legs, mewing loudly.

Martha looked around, but she did not see any mouse. She wondered if perhaps Auld Mary had not seen her yet. But the old woman turned a beaming eye upon her and said, "A red-headed mouse, me favorite kind!" So Martha knew she was the mouse.

She swallowed and said in a small voice, "Good day to you, ma'am."

"Put this on the bench, there's a lass," Auld Mary said, handing Martha a basket that was covered with a handkerchief. "I'll just see to oor liddle bit o' dinner."

Martha could not speak. She set the basket beside the oatcakes, wondering what was inside it. She stood still and watched as Auld Mary took the pot off the fire and poured its contents onto a pile of heather on the dirt floor. The water drained through and soaked into the dirt, leaving four small potatoes steaming on top of the heather.

Auld Mary picked up two knitting needles and used them to lift a potato onto each plate. It seemed to Martha a very odd thing to do. Then she saw that there were no knives or forks on the table.

"Well, be you hungry or be you not?" Auld Mary asked. She motioned for Martha to take a seat on one of the stools. Martha stared. It was almost as if Auld Mary had known she was coming.

People did say Auld Mary had the second sight. Perhaps she really could see into the future. Then she would already know why Martha was here. Suddenly Martha felt a great leap of excitement. Maybe that was what was in the covered basket! Perhaps Auld Mary had already gone out to pick the magic plant that would make Martha grow faster!

Martha felt her shyness melt away. She sat on the stool and hungrily ate the steaming boiled potatoes and the crisp oatcakes.

Talking to Auld Mary was not like talking to anyone else Martha knew. The old woman spoke to the cat as much as to Martha, and she paused and nodded as if he were answering her back. When she did speak to Martha, it was as though Martha dropped by for dinner every day. She asked questions about how things were in the Stone House, and Martha found herself chattering away in reply.

She told Auld Mary about the christening procession, and the letter Mum had gotten from Uncle Harry, saying that he was bringing Aunt Grisell and all the cousins to visit for a whole month in the winter.

Through all this, still Auld Mary had not said anything about what was inside the basket.

"It's wonderin' I am if ye've room in that wee belly for a liddle treat," said Auld Mary.

"A treat!" Martha said, surprised.

"Aye," said Auld Mary. "I up an' picked these as soon as ever I knew ye was comin'." She took the handkerchief off the basket. Martha's heart thumped. Then Auld Mary tipped the basket to show Martha the plump purple berries inside.

"Bilberries?" Martha's voice was very small.

"Sure as day." The wrinkled face beamed at Martha. "Th' season's gettin' a mite long in th' tooth for berries, but I kenned there'd be some late hangers-on in that liddle sheltered holler around back o' th' hill. Hied me there the second I saw yer bonny self trippin' cross th' moor, I did."

"Oh," Martha said. She could not think of anything else to say. She knew she ought to be grateful about the bilberries, but they were just plain ordinary bilberries. They would not make her grow big enough to use the spinning wheel.

And if Auld Mary had the second sight,

she had not used it to know Martha was coming. She had only seen her walking toward the cottage.

"Now ye'll no be tryin' to tell me ye've nae taste for bilberries, Mouse," said Auld Mary suddenly. "All mice likes berries. It must be somethin' else troublin' ye. I wish ye'd tell me and Kitty here what it is. I'm nae great shakes at dishin' oot advice, meself, but Kitty's been around a long time and he kens a thing or two."

The orange cat meowed and jumped into Auld Mary's lap. Suddenly Martha found herself telling the whole story. Auld Mary listened and the cat listened. When Martha was done, the cat licked its paw, nuzzled Auld Mary's chin, and leaped down to the floor. It ran out of the house, its long tail waving straight up in the air.

Auld Mary laughed. "The cowardly beast. Canna face tellin' ye the ill news."

Martha swallowed. "Ill news?"

"Aye," Auld Mary said, but her eyes were twinkling. "He kens there's no a plant nor beast on earth can make a wee lass grow before her time. But—" The uncanny green eyes smiled at Martha. "There's mair than one way to shear a sheep. I'll teach ye to spin as I learned when I was no mair than yer size."

"Truly?" Martha cried.

Auld Mary went to a basket in the corner and rummaged around. She came back with a funny-looking wooden stick that had a round wooden disk at one end.

Auld Mary read the question in Martha's eyes. "'Tis a spindle. When I was a bairn, nivver would ye see a lass oot walkin' wi'oot one. Spun all the time, we did, while we were aye mindin' the cows or takin' the air."

She ran a finger along the spindle's length and smiled fondly at it. Then she held out the spindle to Martha, who took it gingerly. It did not look like much, just an old smooth stick stuck through a wooden circle.

Auld Mary went on. "A month's practice wi' this, Mouse, and ye'll be spinnin' yarn jist as fine as anything yer sister, Grisie, can make on her wheel. And by the time ye've grown big enough to take up the wheel yerself, yer fingers'll ken exactly what to do."

Martha gave a sudden grin. "That'd be grand," she said.

Auld Mary took a bit of brushed, combed wool from the bench near her spinning wheel. She showed Martha how to draw out a few woolly hairs and loop them around a piece of string she had tied onto the spindle, just below the round wooden disk. Auld Mary said the disk was called a whorl.

"The string is just to get ye started," she explained. "Noo watch this."

Holding on to the wool she had looped through the string, Auld Mary let the spindle dangle in the air. With her free hand, she set the spindle spinning. The weight of the whorl kept the spindle twirling like a top. As it turned, it twisted the woolly hairs into one tight piece of thread. Auld Mary gently pulled more hairs out from the bit of wool in her hand—it was just like drawing out the strands of flax from Mum's distaff, Martha realized—and allowed the whirling spindle to continue twisting the strands into thread.

That was all there was to it, Auld Mary said. Then she held Martha's hands to show her how to draw out new strands of wool as she set the spindle spinning again.

The wool was softer than the flax had been, and rather greasy. It took a lot of practice before Martha could do it by herself. Sometimes the thread broke and the spindle fell to the ground. Then Auld Mary had to help Martha loop the thread onto the spindle again.

But before she left Auld Mary's house, Martha had spun enough thread to wind into a small ball. It was very thick thread and had almost as many slubs and wide fuzzy patches as the thread she had spun on Mum's wheel. Auld Mary said not to worry; Martha would soon learn the trick of keeping it smooth and even. Auld Mary said she must keep the ball of thread, and the spindle as well.

"'Twas only yesterday it was tellin' me it had a hankering to travel," she said.

"I don't think spindles can talk," Martha said.

For some reason this made Auld Mary laugh and laugh. "And hoo does a mouse come to ken so much about spindles, when she nivver laid eyes on one before today?"

Martha could not think of an answer. Auld Mary laughed again and reached for the basket of bilberries.

"Ye'd best stick to what ye ken, Mouse—like berries! Come noo, ye must eat these up afore ye scoot on home. Gettin' on toward suppertime, it is, and yer mither will wonder where ye've got to!"

Martha was astonished. The afternoon had gone so quickly. When the berries were gone, she thanked Auld Mary and promised to come visit her again.

All the long way home, Martha tried to practice with the spindle. It was harder to do while she was walking. She would practice and practice, Martha told herself, until she could do it perfectly, even while she was moving about. None of her family could spin thread while walking. Not even Grisie.

THE BOAT

Every day after that, Martha took her wool to the garden and practiced and practiced. She liked the way the spindle whirled in the air like a fairy top. She liked the crinkly feel of the wool. She pretended that Lady Flora was a great lady in a grand old castle with fifteen bedrooms, and Martha was her maidservant spinning fine woolen yarn for the household stores.

The yarn she rolled into a ball was beginning to look like proper thread. Martha could not yet keep the spindle from wobbling out of control while she was walking about, but when she sat still, she could spin yarn that was smooth and straight.

At the end of a month, when Martha had spun enough to wind three balls, Grisie said, "You've enough there to knit up a doll blanket. I'll help you, if you like."

An idea flashed into Martha's head. "I want to make mittens," she said. "For Laird Alroch."

"Truly?" Grisie seemed surprised. Martha nodded her head firmly, and Grisie shrugged. "I suppose you could. You've certainly got enough yarn for it, and a good thick yarn it is. It would make fine, warm mittens. But whatever made you think of giving mittens to Laird Alroch?"

Martha shrugged. She did not want to tell Grisie about the dust-gown, or why she wanted to do something nice for the old laird. "He is coming for Hogmanay, isna he?"

Hogmanay was the biggest celebration of the year. It came on the last day of the year, and there would be singing and feasting until midnight and beyond. Uncle Harry and his family would be visiting then, and Laird Alroch.

"Aye. Still, it's a funny notion. I dinna ken where you get your ideas, Martha."

"From me head," Martha answered.

And so it was that Laird Alroch's mittens were knit with Martha's very own wool. They were warm and sturdy with only a few missed stitches, and the right hand was very nearly the same size as the left. Father tried them on, and said he had no doubt Laird Alroch would be proud to wear them.

"Happen one of these days you'll knit me a pair, lass," he said to Martha. Martha felt very proud, and she wished she could begin work on Father's mittens right away. But first, she had decided to make some for Auld Mary, to thank her for the use of the spindle. And after that, she wanted to make a shawl for Lady Flora to wear for the holidays. Lady Flora must have new clothes for Hogmanay.

Everyone was to have a new suit of clothes for the holidays. Mum sent a load of linen and wool yarns to the weaver in Clachan to be made into different kinds of cloth. There was a lot of dyed green linen that Mum said would be just the thing for Martha's new dress. She said there ought to be enough left over to make a little matching gown for Lady Flora.

"Truly?" Martha squealed.

"Aye, but you'll have the hemming of the skirt yourself."

After the finished cloth came back from the weaver, Mum and Grisie began sewing every day nearly from sunup to sundown. Martha worked beside them, knitting Auld Mary's mittens and then Lady Flora's shawl. Martha's new green dress was soon ready. The high waist was belted with a sash of tartan plaid, with stripes of red and green and gold criss-crossing one another. The little matching gown for Lady Flora had its own wee ribbons around the sleeves and bodice, and there were tiny rosettes above each flounce of the skirt. The gown was so pretty that it was almost a shame to cover it with the woolly shawl Martha had knit, and she decided to put that on the doll only when she took her outside.

It was too cold to spend much time out-doors, though, so everyone stayed close to the fire, telling stories and playing winter games.

Mollie and Nannie were as busy with clean-ing as Mum was with sewing. All the floors must be scoured with sand, and all the furni-ture rubbed with a cloth to make the wood gleam.

Everyone was looking forward to the New Year's Eve celebration. Martha found it hard to think of anything else. There would be singing and dancing and presents and everyone's favorite foods. And the day after, New Year's Day, was Martha's birthday. She would be seven years old. That was one year closer to being old enough to search for the water fairy in Robbie's boat.

One night when Martha went to bed, she got Grisie to help her count the days till Hogmanay. Six more days. Then it was five days, and four, and then three. The day before Hogmanay, Duncan came in, his cheeks red with cold.

"Martha! There you are. You must come

and see what I've made down at the lake."
He went to a chest in the corner and rummaged around until he found a large white handkerchief. "There, 'twill be the very thing. Come on!"

So Martha put on her coat and mittens and hood, and she wrapped the white shawl around Lady Flora's shoulders. With the doll tucked in the crook of her arm, she ran down the stairs behind Duncan.

"Found a bit of wood floating in the lake, I did," Duncan said as they puffed down the hill. "I've rigged it up like a skiff. All it wants is a sail."

On the gravel of the shore was a thick piece of wood as long as Martha's arm. Duncan had tied two sticks together in the shape of a cross. He stuck the cross into a crack in the wood, and that was the mast of the boat. Martha did not think it looked much like a boat, and she said so.

"As if you knew aught about boats!" Duncan cried. "Just you wait until you see it on the water. It ought to have a crew, though.

Happen I'll go back for me tin soldiers."

"You ought to try it on the water first," said Martha.

Duncan tied a bit of string to the mast and carefully set the little boat in the water. It bobbed from side to side but did not sink.

"There!" Duncan cried triumphantly. "She's seaworthy, she is." He gave the boat a shove and watched it sail away from the shore. There was not enough wind to fill the sail, but Duncan held tightly to the string anyway.

"But I want to try her with a crew," he said again. "Do us a favor, Martha, and run back up to the house for me soldiers."

Martha set Lady Flora carefully on a large flat stone so that she could watch the boat sail while Martha was gone.

"Mind she doesna fall off and soil her gown!" she called to Duncan as she ran up the hill and into the house.

Cook was standing at the bottom of the stairs.

"Where have you been? I've got the haggis bag all cleaned and ready." Cook had said

Martha might help her prepare it.

"Oh!" Martha had forgotten about the haggis. Pulling off her coat and mittens, she followed Cook into the kitchen. Duncan would just have to wait for his soldiers.

In a small pot of water over the fire was the stomach of a sheep, which Cook had cleaned well before putting it on to boil. Also in the pot were the sheep's liver, lungs, and heart. They would go into the filling of the haggis, and the stomach-bag would hold it all.

Cook chopped everything into tiny bits, and then she asked Martha to bring her the chunk of beef she had ready on the hearth. Cook minced that as well, then she chopped up a cake of dried animal fat called suet, and some onions.

"Just ye sprinkle some meal over this lot as I mix it," Cook said. Martha stood on tiptoe beside her and let the meal sift out of her hands a little at a time.

Then Cook took the stomach out of the boiling water and drained it well.

"Would ye rather hauld it or stuff it?" she asked Martha.

"Stuff it," Martha answered promptly. It was fun to scoop the meat mixture into the stomach-bag. It was like stuffing a feather pillow, only the meat did not fly out of her hands the way feathers did.

As they worked, Cook sang one of her favorite songs. It was about a young man and his sweetheart, who went out to the rye field to have a talk. The young man told the girl he must go away to seek his fortune. He did not want to leave her but thought it was best.

Cook sang:

"Your father takes o' you great care
Your mither combs your yellow hair
But your sisters say that ye'll get nae share
If ye follow wi' me, a stranger."

In the end the lass decided to go away with her sweetheart, though her father might fret and her mother might frown. The girl got no share of her inheritance, and she never saw her parents or her sisters again. It hardly seemed possible that anyone could go so far from home that she could never get back. Martha could not imagine leaving Mum and Father and never seeing Glencaraid again. She would not like to live anywhere but in her own valley.

Martha didn't like to think of the mother and father in the song missing their lass, but still, she sang with gusto as she and Cook finished stuffing the stomach-bag.

> *"This lad he was a gallant bold,*
> *A brave fellow just nineteen years old.*
> *He's made the hills an' the valleys roar*
> *An' the bonnie lassie she's gane wi' him."*

Just before she closed the opening altogether, Cook pressed on the stomach-bag to get all the air out. Then she sewed it closed and put the whole thing back into the kettle of water.

"There! It wants two hours' boiling, and a

finer haggis ye'll nivver have seen," Cook said. Martha did not see how she could wait until tomorrow to eat it.

Cook said a seedcake would help, and she took one out of a big jar.

"It's a wonder we've no had Duncan in here beggin' seedcakes," Cook said.

"Och, Duncan's soldiers!" Martha cried out. "Supposed to bring them down to the lake, I am."

"His own legs was workin', last time I checked," Cook said tartly.

Martha ran to fetch the soldiers, then raced back to the lake with them in hand. Duncan looked up guiltily when he heard her. It took Martha only a second to see why. Lady Flora was not on her stone chair. She was lying on Duncan's boat, staring up at the sky. Her white cap and green skirt stood out bright as flowers against the gray water.

"Duncan!" Martha screamed. "You get her back here!"

"She's all right," Duncan said. "That's the sturdiest boat ever set sail."

"I dinna care," Martha snapped. "Pull her back in, now."

Duncan began to tug the board back to shore. It had floated a long way out; the string was stretched to its length.

Martha watched anxiously. The boat bobbed from side to side, splashing up little drops of water as it moved.

"Mind her gown!" Martha scolded. "That's her good—"

She choked to a stop in the middle of the sentence. The board had wobbled a bit too far to one side and water rushed up onto its surface.

"It's going to sink!" Martha wailed.

"Nay, I'll not let that happen," Duncan said, but he looked worried. "Just give me a minute's peace to gentle her in."

"But Flora's getting all wet!"

Duncan did not say anything now; he only bit his lip and tugged slowly on the string. But it was no use. The woolen shawl soaked up the water and grew very heavy. The boat sank lower and lower in the water.

"She's going to drown!" Martha cried.

"Nay—" Duncan began, tugging harder on the string. The stick mast suddenly slipped to the side, and the linen handkerchief slumped half in the water and half over Lady Flora's sodden skirt. Now the boat was heavier on one side, and it slowly tilted up, one edge raising out of the water. Lady Flora began to slide.

Martha opened her mouth to shout, but nothing came out. She watched in horror as her doll slid off the board and into the lake.

"Dinna worry," Duncan said, sounding very worried. "Flora canna sink. She's made of wood."

But the heavy dress and wet shawl weighed down the painted piece of wood that was Martha's doll. Slowly Lady Flora sank beneath the water.

Martha rushed forward, but Duncan grabbed her arm and pulled her back.

"Martha, nay! You mustn't. You'll catch your death, and anyhow, you ken you canna swim!"

"I care not!" Martha sobbed. "She'll be drowned!"

"She's drowned already, Martha," Duncan whispered. His voice sounded like crying, too. "I'm sorry, truly I am."

The linen sail and the mast sticks were gone. Lady Flora was gone. All that was left was the wet board, floating light as a leaf now that its passenger had sunk to the bottom of Loch Caraid.

HOGMANAY

Suddenly it was here, the day Martha had been waiting for: Hogmanay—Old Year's Day. Cook was anxious all morning to see if the sun would shine, for that meant good luck in the year to come.

But Martha didn't care if the sun shone or not. She did not see how her luck could get much worse. Lady Flora was gone. She hated to put on her dress that morning when all she could think of was Lady Flora's wee matching one cold and wet at the bottom of the lake.

It was a cold, clear, wintry sky. Like everyone else, the wind was in a hurry today. It pushed Martha from behind and made her run when she went out to watch Mollie air the linens for the guest room.

"Aisy goes it, lass," Mollie scolded. "Here, hauld out yer arms."

Mollie laid the stack of folded sheets on Martha's outstretched arms. Then she took the top sheet off the stack and shook it out vigorously. The sheet flapped in the wind and nearly flew right out of Mollie's grasp. Martha would have liked to do the flapping part, but Mollie said she was too small.

"Indeed," Mollie told her, "yer that small, ye'd likely get carried off by the wind like a schooner w' her sails up!"

Martha did not like to think of boats and sails, for that reminded her of Lady Flora. "No, I wouldna," she said indignantly. "I've got me heavy boots on."

Mollie laughed. "Och, she's her father's daughter, is this one." One by one she shook out the linens, then Mollie took the whole stack and turned back toward the house.

Martha trailed along behind her, feeling as if the long day would never creep toward evening. Everyone was busy. Mum was packing baskets of presents for Father to take to all the tenant families. After dinner, Father took the baskets around to each cottage. Last year, he had taken Alisdair along. This year, he took Grisie, and Robbie, too. Martha had begged to go, but Father said briskly that she and Duncan must stay to help Mum and the servants get ready for the party. Uncle Harry and Aunt Grisell and the cousins would be arriving soon, and so would Laird Alroch.

Duncan was the last person Martha wanted to be left with today. When she saw him beckoning to her from the stable, she turned her back on him and walked furiously toward the house.

"Och, Martha, dinna be cross," he begged. "Please? I told you I was sorry! I'll get you a new doll, I promise!"

"I dinna want it!" Martha yelled, without

turning around. She was too mad. "Lady Flora was the best doll in the world!"

Her cheeks flamed. She would never forgive him, never. She stalked away from him into the house and wandered out to the kitchen. In the center of the noise and bustle was Mum, looking flushed and excited. The bannocks for tonight must be baked by Mum's own hands, to bring good luck to all who ate them. It was a whole afternoon's job, for she must make a lot. All the cottagers and half the village would knock on the door of the Stone House that evening, and no one must be sent away empty-handed. It was a Hogmanay tradition.

Cook hovered over Mum all through the baking. Mum could prepare as fine a meal as Cook could, any day, but Cook hated to see her do it. She worried and fussed and predicted dire happenings. The grease would spatter and stain Mum's gown, or land on her ladyship's dear hands and raise a fearful blister, and her ladyship would miss all the fun that night.

"As if I'd let a blister spoil my Hogmanay!" Mum retorted.

"There you are!" Mum said, spotting Martha. "I wondered where you'd got to. How's my lass this afternoon? Did you make it up with Duncan?"

Martha shrugged her shoulders.

"It's not well to carry a quarrel into the new year," Mum said gently. "Duncan has been punished, and it's truly sorry he is that your bonny doll is lost."

Still Martha said nothing. She climbed onto a stool to watch Mum make the bannocks and Mum gave her a cake, fresh from the pan and stinging hot.

There was a hollow space in her stomach that seemed to choke with tears every time she thought of Lady Flora. How bonny she had looked in her fine holiday gown! But the oatcake had filled a tiny corner of the hollow space, and then the house began to fill with guests, and it was so noisy that Martha could not hear the quiet space inside her.

Uncle Harry arrived first, with his big

family. Their carriage rolled into the court-yard just as Father appeared at the top of the hill. Grisie and Alisdair were just behind him, their faces red from the wind. Grisie ran to greet the cousins as they climbed out of the carriage. She always liked to see Janet and Meg, Uncle Harry's oldest daughters. Mary and Rachel were Martha's age, and there were David and Harold in between, and baby Eamonn in Aunt Grisell's arms.

It was already growing dark, and the wind was far too bitter for standing outside. Every-one hurried into the parlor. There was a loud confusion of coats and shawls being taken off, and peats being heaped on the fire, and Uncle Harry thwacking Father and Alisdair and Robbie on the back, and a great roar of laughter when he thwacked Mum by mis-take.

"She's getting soft, is my sister!" Uncle Harry boomed. "I remember a time when she'd have walloped me right back!"

"I'd wallop you still," Mum said, laughing, "but I fear I'd lay you flat!"

Martha loved to listen to Mum and Uncle Harry tease each other. Mum's cheeks flushed red, and she looked nearly as young as Grisie, laughing up at her big, curly-haired brother.

Then Robbie looked out the window and shouted that another carriage was coming. Laird Alroch had arrived. Sandy went out to help the old laird's driver put away the horses and the carriage.

While Father and Uncle Harry greeted Laird Alroch, Martha slipped into the kitchen to watch the bustle of preparations. Mollie squeezed past her in the doorway, holding high a platter of sliced roast beef in one hand and a tureen of soup in the other.

"Look sharp, Miss Martha," she said cheerily. "Ye dinna want a crock o' broth comin' doon upon ye to muss yer pretty frock!"

The kitchen was a blur of bodies rushing to and fro. The table was filled with dishes of food, some of them waiting to be carried out to the parlor and others to be eaten by the servants when things calmed down a bit. Cook and Mollie and the others would have their own holiday feast in the kitchen.

Uncle Harry's coachman and Laird Alroch's coachman were warming their hands at the fire. Cook gave them each a cup of ale. She had changed into her best clothes, and she was an imposing sight in her black wool dress and her best white apron, so stiffly starched that it crackled when she moved. Her face was redder than ever, and her eyes seemed to look every direction at once. But Martha could see that she was enjoying herself immensely.

Nannie, bright and fresh in her own Sunday frock, smiled at Martha from the kitchen table and beckoned her over for a taste of the almond-cream she was whipping. Eagerly Martha ran to lick the spoon. She closed her eyes and let the sweet, nut-flavored cream melt on her tongue.

"'Tis like a spoonful of cloud," she said to Nannie.

Nannie laughed and said, "Ye'd best flit back to the parlor before Cook puts ye to work, miss!"

"I heard that, Nan Jenkins." Cook's voice boomed over Martha's head. But when Martha turned to look at her, Cook was smiling broadly. She put a hand under Martha's chin. "Och, look at the bonny wee thing in her fine feathers," she said tenderly, admiring Martha's dress. "That green is just the shade to bring oot the fire in yer hair. Noo—off ye go back to the parlor."

With a last wistful glance at the bowl of almond-cream, Martha ran out of the kitchen and back into the parlor. Everything was ready now for the feast. Tall candles flamed above the silver candlesticks in the center of the long parlor table. There was so much food on the table that she could hardly see the tablecloth. There was pigeon pie and boiled lamb, boiled chicken and sheep's-head broth. There were two puddings and three kinds of jelly, and bread and potatoes and a round of venison. There was a rich, tasty haggis. The sideboard groaned beneath its load of desserts.

Father stood at the table and cleared his

throat. It was time for him to say grace. Everyone became quiet. He began the long prayer that thanked God for the bountiful feast and the good health of the family. Martha closed her eyes tight so she would not be tempted to peek at the platters of delicious food.

At last grace was over, and it was time to eat. Nearly every chair was filled at the long table. Uncle Harry joked that he couldn't tell which plate was his to eat off.

Martha, giggling, caught Duncan's eye. He grinned at her eagerly. Once, a long time ago, they had promised each other always to be good friends like Mum and Uncle Harry. But Uncle Harry had never drowned Mum's doll. Martha scowled at Duncan and looked away. She filled the hollow space in her stomach with almond-cream and sweetmeats.

Somehow, though, the hollow space seemed to be growing larger. Martha ate until she had eaten too much, and her stomach felt uncomfortably full. But right on top of that was the aching empty spot. She wanted everything to be like it had been yesterday, when

Lady Flora was in her arms and there was all the excitement of Hogmanay to look forward to. Now that Hogmanay was here, Martha felt cheated. She should be having more fun.

Duncan's eyes were sad. Martha felt angrier when she saw that. She felt as though she were spoiling his holiday, when really it was the other way around. She wished he were not sitting across from her so that she wouldn't have to look at him.

Then supper was over, and Mollie and Nannie came to collect the empty dishes. Mum sat down at the pianoforte. Everyone clustered around her. She began to sing:

> "*I had a wee hen, and I loved it well,*
> *I fed my hen on yonder hill.*"

Everyone joined in.

> "*My hen, chuckie-chuckie, chuckie-*
> *chuckie, coo,*
> *Everyone loves their hen, why should I*
> *not love my hen, too?*"

This was the best part of Hogmanay, the singing—and the presents. Everyone had a present on Hogmanay night. There was even a little package for Tullie Grayshanks.

Mum came into the parlor with a big rush basket. It was filled with mysterious rag bundles. Each bundle was tied around with a ribbon, and the ends of the ribbons trailed out of the basket. There was a name embroidered on each trailing end.

Mum placed the basket in the middle of the room, and there was a mad scramble as each child raced to find the ribbon with his or her name on it. Martha ducked under elbows until she found the fluttering bit of silk with her name on it. It was a dark green ribbon that just matched her dress, and she could use it for her hair later. Martha tugged on the ribbon, trying to follow it to the bundle at its other end. There was a riot of laughter and friendly scuffling as ribbons tangled and cousins collided.

Martha's bundle was long and skinny. She tore off the scrap of cloth. Inside was a pair of knitting needles. They were made of wood, and they were smooth and straight. She had never seen such lovely needles. Their pointed ends were not too sharp, and their other ends were round and flat, so that the loops of yarn would not slip off when she was knitting.

"Oh, Mum!" she said. Mum smiled at her.

"Thank your father, my dear," she said. "He had the choosing of them, when he went to Perth."

Martha gave Father a kiss on the cheek. Duncan gave a shout of joy and came running to thank Father for the new set of paints. Martha brushed past him and ran to show her needles to Rachel and Mary. Then the hollow place inside throbbed a little when she remembered that she could not knit any more wee clothes for Lady Flora. The thought made her scowl.

"Such a grim face for such a bonny lass," Laird Alroch said, ruffling her hair. His kind eyes twinkled down at her.

Martha remembered the present she had made him. She ran to the sideboard and grabbed the soft package. Feeling shy, she held it out to Laird Alroch.

"What's all this, then?" said the old laird. He unwrapped the package and took the two gloves into his hands. There was a look of wonder on his face.

"Spun the wool and knit them meself, I did," Martha said.

Laird Alroch put a hand on Martha's cheek. Suddenly she threw her arms around his neck and hugged, hard.

Now there was more singing, and soon came a knock at the door.

"Quick, the bannocks!" Mum cried. Someone pushed a basket into her hands and she moved swiftly to open the door.

"Hurrah!" cried the crowd of boys standing in the chill night air. Their noses and cheeks were pink, and their breath made frosty clouds around their faces. They sang in rough, cheery voices:

> *"Get up, gude wife, and binna sweer,*
> *An' deal yer bread to them that's here,*

For the time'll come whan ye'll be dead,
An' then ye'll need neither ale nor bread."

Martha crowded close to watch. She thought it would be fun to join them, to go singing at the doors of every house on the estate. Her brothers and the boy cousins were putting on their caps. They could go, because they were boys. Even Duncan was allowed to go. It did not seem fair that she and Grisie must stay home.

Mum handed the basket around. Each boy took one oatcake, and then Mum said they might each take another. There were so many baskets of cakes still in the kitchen. Martha slipped her hand in and took an oatcake as the basket went past, and Mum pretended not to notice.

It was very late now, but Martha was not at all tired. She wanted to stay awake till midnight, to see who would be first foot. The first person to set foot in the house after midnight would have extra good luck in the new year. There was a lot of joking and guessing about who it would be this year. Uncle Harry said it was sure to be his son David, and Father was certain it would be Robbie. It could not be Alisdair, because of his red hair. It would bring very bad luck upon the whole household if the first foot was a redhead. No one could explain to Martha why that was so.

Grisie played the pianoforte, and then Mum made Martha play a little tune. Laird Alroch clapped and clapped and said he'd nivver heard such fine playing in all his days.

Uncle Harry sang a song about Finn MacChumhail and the lady giant who taught him to forge iron. Aunt Grisell told the story of the time Bonnie Prince Charlie had spent the night in her brother's room, long ago when she was a little girl living far away in the north.

Laird Alroch began a tale. His wavery voice flickered up and down like the fire. Martha felt herself staring very hard at the fire, and then her head was resting on Grisie's lap, and Grisie was stroking her hair. She was sure she was still wide awake. But things seemed to swirl around before her eyes and all the stories got mixed up together. The lady giant was telling Prince Charlie not to worry, Lady Flora was not turned to stone. She had only gone to live in Loch Caraid with the water fairy. The water fairy would not be lonely now that she had a bonny doll to love.

Suddenly everyone was standing and Father was taking out the green glass bottle of claret wine, and Martha knew that it was midnight already. She could not remember the end of Laird Alroch's story. But if she closed her eyes she could see the water fairy combing the long floating strands of Lady Flora's hair with a willow twig. She wanted to see the water fairy more than ever now, to know if she really was taking care of Flora.

Father poured a glass of claret for each of the adults. It was toasting time. Father held up his glass.

"May the good Lord hold us all in His hand, this year and always," he said in his low, solemn voice.

"Aye," said Uncle Harry, raising his glass.

"Finer words nivver were spoken," said Laird Alroch. Everyone took a drink. Martha pretended her tea was claret, but she didn't know what claret tasted like. She thought it must be sour, because Grisie pursed her lips in a funny way after she took a sip. This was the first year Grisie was allowed a glass of the wine.

Now it was Mum's turn. She lifted her glass and made her toast.

"May our hearts be filled with love, our minds with wisdom, and our bodies with health."

"Och, me lass," said Laird Alroch, "finer words nivver were spoken."

Uncle Harry said in his booming voice, "May the wind of sorrow ne'er blow open our door."

"Finer words nivver were spoken, me boy," croaked Laird Alroch. Cousin Mary gave Martha a nudge. Every year, Laird Alroch said the same thing about every single toast. Martha choked back a giggle.

Grisie spoke up shyly. "May our fires burn bright and our water run clear." Her voice could hardly be heard. Martha could not wait till she was old enough to make a toast. She would make certain that everyone heard her.

When it came Laird Alroch's turn, he gave Mum a long, beaming look before speaking.

"May blessings rain down upon this fine lady, as she pours them oot on those around her," he said. Mum's eyes grew suddenly glistening.

"Finer words were never spoken, sir," said Father seriously. He looked into Mum's eyes and drained his glass. For a moment the hollow space in Martha's middle rose to her throat in a great happy lump. She was glad to be her particular self in this particular family. There could be no nicer family in all the world than Father and Mum, and Grisie and Alisdair and Robbie and—Duncan.

The happy lump dropped back into her middle and became a cold hollow space again.

Just then came another loud knock at the door. Everyone jumped and laughed. The first foot had come. There was a hush in the air while everyone waited to see who it would be.

"Great lairds of thunder!" cried Uncle Harry.

The door had opened upon Duncan. He was panting as if he had run very hard.

He stepped inside and held out a bottle and a little cloth sack. It was another Hogmanay custom that the person who set first foot inside the house must bring certain gifts: whiskey, bread, a little salt.

After the first surprised silence, there was a roar of greeting. Father gave Duncan a little clap on the back.

"You've made clever work, my lad, to beat out your brothers," he said.

"And my David!" roared Uncle Harry approvingly.

"Where be they?" Father asked. "Still carousing in the cottages?"

"I canna say, Father," Duncan said. He was still out of breath. "I—I didna go with them. I had—an errand to run."

"What's this?" Father asked, drawing his brows together in the beginnings of his stern look.

"Peace, Allan," Mum said lightly. She ushered Duncan inside and hurried him to the fire. When he spoke, his words tumbled over each other. He said that he had gone to Auld Mary's cottage. Father and Mum were surprised. It was a long walk in the daytime, and now it was a bitter cold and rainy night.

"You must be frozen through, lad!" Mum exclaimed.

"Auld Mary gave me some soup," Duncan said. "She had it waiting for me. Said she was expecting me, she did!"

Mum and Father exchanged a look. A chill went down Martha's spine. Had Auld Mary really known Duncan was coming? Perhaps she did have the second sight after all.

"But why ever did you go there, boy?" Father said sternly. "Miles across the moor, alone, at night!"

Duncan looked nervous but resolute. "I had to, sir," he said. "Wanted to make it up to Martha, I did, for losing her doll on the loch. You ken Auld Mary makes dolls. I thought she could trade me one for my new paint set."

Martha's mouth dropped open. She heard Mum gasp. Duncan had gone all the way across the moor to sell his brand-new paints! He had wanted those paints for months.

"But she didn't have any," he went on, "at least not the kind I was thinking of. But she gave me this." He turned to Martha and thrust a bundle into her arms.

"It's nothing like your fine Lady Flora, Martha," he said. "I don't ken as you'll care for it at all. But Auld Mary said you'd like it."

Martha stared at the bundle. She felt dazed. It was a scrap of coarse hand-spun flannel wrapped around something hard. Duncan watched her with anxious eyes.

Slowly she unwrapped the bundle. It was a small, plain wooden box. The top of the box lifted off. Inside were a tiny wooden table and two tiny chairs. The backs of the chairs and the legs of the table were carved with the most delicate little vines and dainty flowers. The chair seats were woven from oat-straw. There was a cauldron made of a hollowed-out acorn. There was a wee cradle with rockers on the bottom. It rocked on Martha's palm when she picked it up. Inside the cradle was the tiniest of babies, with a muslin head and a little soft body all wrapped in silk.

Best of all were the mother and father dolls. They too were made of muslin, and their eyes and mouths were bits of bright thread. The mother doll wore a dress of gauzy blue, with a cunning little hat that looked exactly like a bluebell. The father doll had brown knee breeches and a green blouse, and his cap was apple red. Both dolls had pointed muslin ears.

"Oh, Duncan," Martha whispered. She had never seen anything so lovely in her life.

"Auld Mary says it belonged to a fairy's bairn," said Duncan. "She found it on the moor the night after the fairies' last dance. She says the Wee Folk won't take back a toy after it's been lost, and so she brought it home, and then a cock crowed three times and so she kenned it was meant for you."

"Your paints," Martha said in a tiny voice.

"Auld Mary wouldna take them," said Duncan. "She said she'd not trade for what she'd only found. But I'm to paint a picture for her, she says."

"What about the whiskey and the salt?" Father asked. He did not like to take things without paying for them.

"She made me take them, Father," said Duncan. "She said it would bring good luck on her for the giving."

Father nodded, accepting. "We must all go over tomorrow to thank her," said Mum.

Before anyone else could speak, there came a pounding at the door. It was Alisdair, Robbie, and David, all out of breath and jostling to be in front. Uncle Harry burst into his great roaring laugh, and that set everyone else laughing. None of them could be first foot, for Duncan had beaten them to it.

The hollow space in Martha's middle was filling—with Uncle Harry's booming laughter, and Mum's light, high laugh like the rippling of a brook, and the proud, smiling glow in Father's eyes. It was filling with the good luck of the New Year, the miles of windy moor between the Stone House and Auld Mary's rough cottage, the noise and teasing of her brothers and sister and cousins. It was filling with Duncan's happy grin. It was full—it was gone. There was no hollow space inside. There was only a good sort of ache that made her want to hug Duncan.

"You're a grand brother." She whispered it, but everyone heard. "I'm glad I'm your sister."

"Finer words, lass," said old Laird Alroch, "nivver were spoken."

BEYOND THE PAGES OF
LITTLE HOUSE
IN THE HIGHLANDS

HISTORY

IN MARTHA'S TIME

Martha Morse was born in 1782 in Scotland. What was happening in America around that time?

1776 • Declaration of Independence signed

1781 • U.S. wins the War of Independence

1787 • U.S. Constitution signed

1789 • George Washington inaugurated as first U.S. President

1790 • Washington, D.C., founded
U.S. population 3.7 million

1791 • Bill of Rights approved

1793 • Eli Whitney invents the cotton gin

1796 • English physician Edward Jenner introduces vaccination against smallpox

1797 • John Adams inaugurated as second U.S. President

1800 • U.S. government moves to Washington, D.C.

Song

"Tam o' the Linn"
A Traditional Scottish Folk Song

Tam o' the Linn came up the gate,
Wi' twenty puddings on a plate
And each pudding had a preen.
"We'll eat them all," said Tam o' the Linn.

Tam o' the Linn had no breeches to wear,
So he coft him a sheep's skin to make him a pair,
The skinny side out, the woolly side in,
"It's grand summer clothin'," said Tam o' the Linn.

Tam o' the Linn went over the moss,
To seek a stable for his horse.
The moss was open, and Tam fell in—
"I've stabled meself!" cried Tam o' the Linn.

GAME

JACKSTRAWS

This is a game like our own pick-up sticks, played during Martha's time. It requires a very steady hand. Players 2+ (You can always practice on your own.)

1. Collect a bunch of thin sticks from your yard or use some straws from your kitchen.
2. Make a pile of the sticks or straws by holding them in your hand and dropping them on the floor or a table.
3. Remove one stick or straw at a time without disturbing any others.
4. The player's turn continues until a stick is moved.
5. Each player that removes a stick or straw successfully gets a point. The player with the most points wins.

RECIPE

PORRIDGE

The smell of warm porridge had filled the air along with Mollie's song. Martha slid open the door-panel and climbed out of bed. . . . The good porridge smell chased the last sleepiness out of the room.

One of Martha's favorite foods was porridge. Here's how to make it!

1 CUP OATMEAL	½ CUP CREAM
4 CUPS WATER	SAUCEPAN
2 TEASPOONS SUGAR	SPOON

1. Put the oatmeal in a pot, and add the water.
2. Over medium heat, stir the oatmeal and water until it starts to simmer (ask an adult for help with this).
3. Lower the heat and keep stirring for five minutes.
4. Mix in the sugar and the milk.
5. Serve and enjoy! For an added treat, drizzle honey on top!

STORY

Martha loved it when Mum told her stories—especially fairy stories!

THE CROFTER'S DAUGHTER AND THE WEDDING DRESS

There once was a poor crofter who farmed a small bit of land in a bare stony glen. He had a light heart and a merry way about him.

As men will do, he had married a wife who was as like to him as wet is to dry. Never was there a moment when she was not all a-flutter with worry over this and over that. Most of all she worried that her daughter would never find a husband.

Now, this daughter was as bonny a lass as the hills had ever seen. She had her father's way of looking for the good in a thing, and over and over she did tell her mother not to worry about a silly thing like a husband.

"If I'm to marry, a husband will find me," she would say to her mother, "as sure as rain finds its way to the soil."

"Husbands dinna fall from the sky like rain!"

her mother would cry.

"Aye, and 'tis a good thing," laughed the lass, "for whatever we'd do with them all after a storm, I canna say!"

Sure and that girl was right not to worry, for it was just that laughter rippling down the hillside that caught the ear of a young man on his way across the valley. When he caught sight of the lass, with her merry eyes and her shining red hair, he said to himself: There's the very girl for me. He introduced himself to the mother, and pointed out that they were to be neighbors of a sort. Then he asked if he might have a drink of water before he headed up the mountain to the farm waiting for him on the other side.

A week later he was back again, and every week after that, and so it was no surprise to the mother that a day came when the lad asked the crofter for the daughter's hand in marriage. The crofter knew the lad well by this time and was aye glad to see his daughter make such a fine match. So the lad and lass were happy, and the crofter was happy, and the mother ought to have been the happiest of all.

But as soon as the wedding plans were made, the mother's worries began again about how she should ever find the means to make her daughter's wedding dress. There was hardly enough flax that year to spin linen for sheets, and as the girl pointed out to her mother, a bride must have at least one set of sheets to carry to her husband's house. And a dress could not be bought either, for coins were scarce as hen's teeth in the crofter's house.

The lass vowed to herself that she would find a way to make a wedding dress that would cheer her mother's heart.

She went out along on the hillside to think about it. She took her spindle out of her pocket and tried to twist a few blades of grass into yarn, but that didna work. She tried with some heather, but that didna work.

In the end she threw herself down in the grass and might even have cried from the hopelessness of it, if a wee strange noise had not come to her ear. It was a sound a bit like a cricket chirping and a bit like a bird peeping, and most of all like someone crying.

To her great surprise, there in the gorse bush was a tiny, tiny lass, weeping her poor heart out. The crofter's daughter saw at a glance that she was one of the Wee Folk. The beautiful fair lass wore a bodice of golden silk, bright as the sun, and a blue skirt of a cloth that rippled to the ground like water flowing over stones. Her shawl was of lacy white gauze, so light and airy that it danced around the fairy in a cloud as she sobbed.

"Whatever is the matter?" asked the crofter's lass.

"'Tis my wedding day a month from now, and I've nothing to wear but this old sorry frock I've worn for more seasons than a mortal could count!" the fairy said.

"But it's lovely!" gasped the crofter's daughter. "Nivver in my life have I seen a gown so fine!"

The fairy's eyes filled with scorn, and a scornful hand plucked at her bodice. "Anyone can snatch a few sunbeams and spin them into yarn."

The crofter's daughter gasped again. "It canna be possible! And your skirt?"

"Water, of course," said the fairy impatiently. "And my shawl is spun from a bit of wind, as any fool can see. Any fairy worth her mettle must think of something that's never been turned into cloth before. I was going to spin the thread out of fire, but I've just found out my groom can't abide the smell of smoke! Am I to have him sneezing all over me at the wedding feast, then?" She burst into a fresh round of sobs.

The crofter's daughter bit her lip, thinking. "I

hope I'm no makin' too bold," said the lass, "but happen ye could have your flame-colored gown after all. By chance would a lock of my hair serve as thread for your cloth?"

Now it was the fairy's turn to gasp, and she stared at the lass in wonder. The lass's red hair with the sun glinting upon it did indeed glow like fire.

"'Twould be the very thing," murmured the fairy, and a smile lit up her face.

So the lass cut off a lock of her hair and tied it fast with a bit of thread. She gave it to the fairy, saying, "Take it, and I wish you as much joy in your marriage as I hope to find in mine."

"Are you to be married also?" cried the fairy. "Then you must let me help with your wedding dress! I can spin you the thread in the blink of an eye!"

And sure enough, the fairy reached up and caught hold of a sunray. She took out a little spindle, and quicker than quick, she turned that sunbeam into a shimmering golden thread. Then she dipped her hand into the stream and brought some of the clean, cool water to her spindle producing a skein of thread as blue as a summer lake. And at the last, she simply held the spindle in the air and let it spin around in the breeze, spinning a skein of airy white thread.

"For your veil," said the fairy, and she gave all the thread to the lass. Then, taking up the flame-red lock of hair, the fairy said good-bye to the girl and *pop*! she disappeared.

The girl took her thread home to her mother and told her all about the wee fairy. The mother was amazed, and when she had woven the thread into cloth she shook her head in wonder, for never was there a mortal bride more lovely than the crofter's daughter. After that the crofter's wife made up her mind not to fret and worry anymore. Who could be fretful with a daughter so sweet and merry that she charmed even the fairy folk?

THE FAR SIDE OF THE LOCH
by MELISSA WILEY

ON THE GLASS MOUNTAIN

The Stone House, which had been so crowded and jostling earlier in the winter, seemed all empty corners now. All day Martha's mother and sister worked quietly at their spinning, their knitting, their sewing. Mum was not herself; she was waiting tensely for Father's next letter.

Nearly three months had passed since Father had left the valley of Glencaraid in the company of Uncle Harry and his big family.

Uncle Harry and Aunt Grisell and the cousins had come to the Stone House in late December for a long visit, and while they were there, the house had been as crowded as a sheep-yard in spring. There had been hardly a single corner of the house that someone was not using to sleep or read or sew or eat in. Cook had complained that it was like living in a thunderstorm, but Martha loved every noisy, bustling minute of it. Then Father and Uncle and Aunt and all the cousins had packed up and said good-bye, and without them it did seem as though a great storm had swept through the Stone House and left everything flattened and changed in its wake.

Terribly changed—for Father had taken Martha's two oldest brothers with him. It was time, he said, for Alisdair and Robbie to get some schooling of a higher quality than that offered by the little village school in Clachan across the lake. So Father enrolled them in a boarding school in faraway Edinburgh, where their cousins David and Harold were pupils. Mum said they would not come home until the summer holidays, and then only for a few weeks.

Martha could hardly believe it was true. Alisdair gone—Alisdair with his kind, absentminded smile and his store of interesting things to talk about—there was not another soul in the valley who knew as much about steam engines and spinning mills and the revolutions of America and France. Martha ached with missing him, and with missing Robbie, too. Robbie stirred things up; he made sparks fly.

At least Duncan, the youngest brother, had not been sent to Edinburgh yet. He was not yet nine; Father said another year at home would do him no harm. Even so, Duncan hardly ever *was* home. He still had to go to the village school across the lake. He left the Stone House before dawn and did not come home until suppertime.

Sometimes during the long, quiet winter days, Martha had said to herself that Duncan might as well be in Edinburgh, she saw so little of him. But in the evenings when he came in, puffing and half frozen from his walk around the lake, she took the thought back. It was better to see him for little bits of the day than not to see him at all.

LITTLE HOUSE

LITTLE HOUSE. BIG ADVENTURE.

Little House in the Highlands

It's 1788, and Martha lives in a little stone house in Glencaraid, Scotland. Martha's father is Laird Glencaraid, and the life of a laird's daughter is not always easy for a lively girl like Martha. She would rather be running barefoot through the fields of heather than acting like a proper lady! But between lessons, Martha always finds time to play on the rolling Scottish hills.

Little House by Boston Bay

It's 1814, and Charlotte lives with her family near the city of Boston. What an exciting time she has! There's Mama's garden to tend to, Papa's blacksmith shop to visit, and lots of brothers and sisters to play with. Best of all, Charlotte is a brand-new American girl, born just one generation after the United States of America was formed.

Little House in Brookfield

It's 1845, and Caroline Quiner lives in t... bustling frontier town of Brookfie... Wisconsin. It's been one whole year si... Caroline's father was lost at sea, and eve... member of her family must pitch in to he... with the farm chores. With trips to tow... getting through the first frost, and starti... school, Caroline is busy discovering ne... things every day!

Little House on Rocky Ridge

It's 1893, and Rose and her parents, Lau... and Almanzo, are moving to Missouri, ... land of the Big Red Apple. They say goo... bye to Ma and Pa Ingalls and Laura's s... ters, and set off for the lush green vall... of the Ozarks. The journey is long a... holds many adventures along the w... which they hope will lead them to a n... home and a new life.

HarperCollins*Children'sBooks*

www.littlehousebooks.com